claws of death
Fatal Food Festival Mysteries
Book One

cathy wiley

CLAWS OF DEATH

A Fatal Food Festival Mystery

Cathy Wiley

www.cathywileyauthor.com

Copyright © 2023 by Cathy Wiley

All rights reserved. No part of this publication may be reproduced, distributed, or transmitted in any form or by any means, including photocopying, recording, or other electronic or mechanical methods, without the prior written permission of the author, except as permitted by U.S. copyright law or in the case of brief quotations in articles and reviews.

Cover design by Lisa Firth

This is a work of fiction. All of the names, characters, organizations, places, and events portrayed in this novel are either products of the author's imagination or are used fictitiously. Any resemblance to real or actual events, locales, or persons, living or dead, is entirely coincidental.

All rights reserved.

Published in the United States by Cathy Wiley.

❀ Created with Vellum

To Joe, for his love and support
To Sharon, for her friendship and support

contents

Chapter One	1
Chapter Two	10
Chapter Three	16
Chapter Four	23
Chapter Five	30
Chapter Six	36
Chapter Seven	42
Chapter Eight	53
Chapter Nine	60
Chapter Ten	65
Chapter Eleven	68
Chapter Twelve	76
Chapter Thirteen	84
Chapter Fourteen	91
Chapter Fifteen	100
Chapter Sixteen	109
Chapter Seventeen	116
Chapter Eighteen	125
Chapter Nineteen	133
Chapter Twenty	142
Chapter Twenty-One	146
Chapter Twenty-Two	151
Thank you for reading my book!	155
Recipes	157
Acknowledgments	161
About the Author	163

chapter one
...

I THOUGHT my life couldn't get any worse. Evidently, the universe took that as a challenge.

Wasn't it bad enough that my career as a celebrity chef had reached such an all-time low that the best possible gig was judging cook-offs at a Texas crab festival? And to add insult to injury, it wasn't even a renowned festival, but a knockoff version held in the obscure town of Redding Beach, Texas.

I'd taken small comfort, assuming that in such a minuscule place, I wouldn't run into anyone I knew. No such luck. Because there—across the cavernous canopy tent—stood my least favorite person in the world, Heather Curtis. Ugh. Hoping to avoid her, I pivoted one hundred eighty degrees and tried to walk quickly out of the tent. I'd have sprinted if it wouldn't have been obvious. Ten feet to go. Five feet.

"Jackie Norwood!" Heather shrieked my name.

Shoot. I'd been so close to escaping.

Stopping short and plastering on a fake smile, I turned as Heather sauntered over on orange stilettos. The shoes were a perfect color match to her skin-tight halter dress. As a pale-skinned blonde, I could never pull off that color, but I suppose it worked with her tanned skin and long brown hair. She finally caught up to me. "Well, if it isn't Jacqueline Norwood. I haven't seen you in forever."

I wish.

"It has been a while," I agreed. "Last October, maybe?" The fact of the matter was, I knew exactly when we'd last interacted. She did too. We'd competed on the competitive cooking show *Hacked*, where I'd beaten her in the final round. I was proud of the victory. Not proud of…the other stuff.

She sneered. "Yes. Your win was impressive, considering the amount of alcohol in your system." Heather snagged two champagne flutes from a passing waiter. She swiveled back and shoved a glass in my face. "Champagne?" Her voice was syrupy sweet, but her brown eyes glinted with malice.

I swallowed hard. The temptation was there. The temptation was always there. But I was stronger than that. "No, thanks." I smiled as genuinely as I could, not wanting to give her the satisfaction of getting under my skin.

She shrugged, set the offered glass on a bussing tray, and sipped from the remaining one. "Your loss. It's quite elegant."

I wanted to ask why she was here, but I'd learned over the years not to get Heather talking about herself. She'd never stop. Heather and I had been competitors, rivals even, for almost a decade, since our early days at the CIA. No, not that one. The Culinary Institute of America in California. We'd started at the same time, but success had come more easily for me. I graduated first in our class. Heather had been second. I became a sous chef first, an executive chef first, owned my own restaurant first, and I was the first to be featured and then have my own show on the Gourmet Channel. I was recognized wherever I went and had been in negotiations for my own line of cookware. I was at the pinnacle of my career.

Or I had been—until alcohol knocked me all the way down. I gazed longingly at Heather's champagne while she glanced around the tent, probably ensuring everyone was watching her.

I took a deep breath and focused on our surroundings, searching for something distracting to talk about—anything to make two minutes pass so I could bow out of this conversation politely. Over the cloying odor of Heather's vanilla perfume, I could smell the briny aroma of crab. It was a crab festival, after all. In fact, there were crabs everywhere: crab wind chimes jingling in the breeze; electric crab lights; crab figurines on the rented tables, staring with unblinking eyes at the folding chairs and a giant banner announcing *Welcome to Redding Beach's 1st Annual Crab Festival!* There were crab traps, stuffed crabs, crab tablecloths, crab cups, crab plates, crab swizzle sticks, and—as if they hadn't taken the theme far enough—one giant bright-orange papier-mâché crab hanging from the top, almost as wide as the tent. Orange overload.

Wait a minute...I shifted my gaze from the giant crab to Heather, then back to the crab. I rolled my eyes. "Wait, you matched your outfit to crabs?" I asked her.

"Of course. Unlike some, I enjoy adding color and creativity to my outfits."

I'll admit, I had opted for the classic and perhaps mundane choice of the little black dress paired with dressy flip-flops—with gold sequins to class it up—and hair in a simple top bun. That was my go-to outfit for an occasion like this.

As part of my contract, I was scheduled to engage in the customary meet-and-greet with the lucky guests who'd paid an extra fee to attend the exclusive Friday evening VIP reception. It served as a prelude to the much-anticipated cooking competition scheduled to commence at six p.m. My brother and I had arrived late for the opening ceremony, barely catching the tail end of it. Then, when it was time to mingle, my introverted brother had gone off by himself, leaving me to network. I'd been enjoying it until Heather had shown up. I was about to make an excuse to get away from Heather by feigning a need to find the ladies' room when Heather spoke first.

"So," she said, wiping some condensation from her glass. "How's Simon?"

My entire body tensed. That wasn't an innocent question. Simon Levenson was my husband, with an emphasis on the was. Despite our vows to take each other for better or for worse, Simon hadn't been willing to wait for me to get through my latest stint at rehab. We were still legally married but negotiating divorce terms. Since the split had been all over the tabloids, Heather had to be aware and was just asking to irritate me. It worked.

"Can't say I know, or care, for that matter," I finally responded.

"I guess you can't keep a husband any better than you can keep a cooking show. Or a restaurant."

I took a step closer to her. "At least I had a husband."

She inhaled sharply. "Are you sure—"

A teenage girl clutching a notepad to her chest was suddenly upon us, interrupting Heather's retort. The redheaded young woman wore jeans and a T-shirt with a picture of a crab and the phrase, "I got crabs at Redding Beach." "Ms. Curtis, could you sign my autograph book?" the young woman breathed out.

I don't know how the girl missed the waves of tension emanating from Heather and me. But from the dazed expression in her green eyes, I recognized her as a star-struck fan. And since she was laser-focused on Heather, I knew which star she was struck by. I wouldn't mind striking Heather myself.

Heather preened at the attention. "I'd be happy to." She pulled a pen from her clutch—orange-colored, naturally. I wondered if the pen had orange ink.

The girl, who looked familiar to me, smiled brilliantly. "Oh, thank you."

I took a look at her VIP badge, wondering how someone her age had enough money to pay the additional charge to mingle with the guests and competitors. When I saw her name, it all came back. I did know her: Skylar Brooks. She'd followed me to every event in California. A sweet girl. I'd been super flattered and dubbed her my Super Fan. I guess she'd moved on after I'd moved down and out.

Skylar bounced on her toes while she waited for Heather to sign the book. As soon as Heather passed it back, the girl edged away, avoiding my gaze. "Thank you again."

During Skylar's flight, she bumped into a man in a dark suit before disappearing altogether. She might have been embarrassed to know she'd collided with the mayor.

Thomas Wheeler, the head honcho of Redding Beach, strode in our direction, a cameraman in his wake. The mayor looked every inch the politician: slicked-back dark hair, pin-striped gray suit, shiny black shoes. Seemed rather warm for a muggy May evening. He caught my gaze and smiled, revealing bright-white teeth. "Ms. Norwood, good to see you."

"Hello again, Mayor Wheeler."

"Please, call me Mayor Tom. You know, almost like the song. Ground control and all that." He smiled again.

I did know the song, which quickly got stuck in my head. "Hopefully, you'll have a better outcome than the major did."

He blinked. Maybe he didn't know all of the lyrics. "Anyway, look at my two gorgeous celebrity judges. Greg, take a photo of me between these two beauties," he said to the cameraman, who had a badge that identified him as being from the Gourmet Channel. Tom tried to slip between Heather and me, but I'd already grabbed his shoulder and turned him to face me.

"What do you mean your *two* celebrity judges?"

Heather reached for Mayor Tom's other shoulder, transforming him into our personal wishbone, ready to be snapped apart. "Calm down, Jackie. We weren't certain if you'd even be out of rehab for Tom's crab festival. Worried that you'd flake out on another of your obligations, I volunteered to judge."

My stomach twisted in knots. I'd been out of rehab for six weeks. No way anyone should have wondered if I'd make it here today. But Heather wasn't wrong. It pained me to the core to admit it, but I had a history of being unreliable. I had, in fact, "flaked out" more than once.

Realizing my jaw hurt from clenching, I utilized a relaxing breathing exercise taught at rehab and released my grip on the mayor. "How thoughtful. And how fortunate for you, Mayor Tom."

He rubbed at his shoulder. "Yes. Well, I was excited about the publicity we'd get having two Gourmet Channel stars here. With the two of you and my wife, we'll have three beautiful and qualified judges."

"Well, *one* star." Heather tossed her brown hair behind her shoulders. "One of us lost her show."

Temporarily, I thought to myself. Heather sure knew how to turn the screws. Losing the show had been devastating. The Gourmet Channel executives put up with my antics for a while but eventually grew tired of me showing up late and/or drunk to the set of *Dinner, Drinks, and Decadence*. When my blood alcohol content ended up higher than my ratings, they cancelled the rest of the season.

To add insult to injury, they filled my time slot with Heather's show, *The Clean Cook*. She specialized in gluten-free, dairy-free, and nut-free cooking. I hated to admit it, but that was a clever hook. It seemed everyone was allergic to something or avoided ingredients for dietary reasons. I'd prepared some of the recipes from her show and been impressed despite myself. She was very adept at creating recipes that tasted good without flour, butter, or cream. Like many chefs, I used those ingredients to add richness to a dish. At least I never lowered myself to the overuse of truffle oil.

Now, Heather Curtis was more famous than I was. But I hadn't given up. I was just starting to claw my way back up from rock bottom. One day, I'd have a show on the Gourmet Channel again. One small step at a time. One small judging gig at a time.

"I'm delighted to share a stage with Heather again," I told the mayor. "Hopefully, it'll go better for her this time." I turned, put my arm around the mayor, and smiled.

The Gourmet Channel cameraman/photographer, whose name tag stated he was Greg Wright, looked unaffected by our drama show. I hoped he hadn't filmed it. He snapped several pictures before lowering the camera and waving a hand at us. "Can we switch to have Ms. Norwood in the middle? I like the composition better, putting the pretty blonde between the two brunettes."

Joy. I switched places with the mayor. I suspected the pictures wouldn't come out well since we were all uncomfortable and unhappy. Greg snapped a few photos, frowned at the preview screen, took a couple more, then gave up. "Thank you, ladies, mayor," he said. As he walked away, he gave me a quick wink.

I was pleased, honestly. Greg was gorgeous, in a nerdy way: tousled, curly dark hair, circular silver-rimmed glasses, ripped jeans. Most flattering, he was probably five years or so younger than me. Considering I'd hit the big three-zero while in rehab, I was feeling old and anxious. Being served divorce papers on my birthday hadn't helped.

I sighed. Needing comfort, I aimed toward the one person I could trust. I might have lost out in my career and my marriage, but I'd certainly won the brother lottery. Daniel was the only one who'd stood by me in the last year. Not even our parents had stuck by me, although they'd been happy with the money I'd thrown at them during the flush years.

Not surprisingly, Daniel was off by himself in a corner, cell phone in hand, probably reading one of his favorite mystery novels. VIP event or not, he was as dressed up as he ever got, in jeans and a dark polo shirt. He glanced up and stood, tucking the phone into his jeans pocket as I approached.

"Hey, little brother," I said, looking up at him. I always enjoyed calling him that. He was two years younger than me, but at six-two, he was four inches taller and over a hundred pounds heavier.

"Hey, big sister. I saw that nasty woman offering you champagne. I'm impressed you resisted."

"It was hard to turn down, actually," I admitted. "You know how I loved champagne."

"Oh no, not that. You're already proving you can resist that. I'm impressed you resisted slapping her into next week."

I laughed, easing the tension I'd felt since spotting Heather. Daniel had always been talented at fixing my bad moods, usually with humor.

It was also uplifting to hear his confidence in my willpower. "I'm glad you're so sure of my ability to resist. I'm still surprised it's working this time, considering I failed rehab before. Twice."

"Well, the third time is the charm, obviously. And you didn't have April those other times." He laughed, shaking his head. "That woman is a force unto herself."

That accurately described April Yao, my Alcoholics Anonymous sponsor, the most strong-willed woman I'd ever met. But even April couldn't rid me of my Heather problem. I explained to Daniel how Heather had wormed her way in as a judge.

"Well, you can outcook her, outlook her, and outshine her on the screen. I'm sure you'll outjudge her too." Daniel looked across the tent to where the preparation and judging area was set up. "How many contestants are you judging?"

I shrugged. "Not sure. I haven't had a chance to check the list yet, although I am curious." The mayor's ambitious plan for the festival was a crab soup competition this evening, crab cakes tomorrow at noon, and something he called crab freestyle Sunday evening. That night, chefs could prepare whatever they wanted, as long as it contained blue crab. "I'll probably be sick of seafood by the end of this weekend. I suspect I'll end up a little crabby."

Daniel rolled his eyes at my pun as we headed to the front left of the tent. The area was full with over a dozen soup kettles and slow cookers on folding tables. A few chefs, including one with a hair color that rivaled Heather's dress, were chopping up last-minute garnishes, releasing the grassy smell of herbs into the air. Most of the initial cooking of their soups had been done at nearby restaurants, in RVs, in food trucks, or in tents on what I knew would be temporary and often temperamental equipment.

The smells were a tantalizing delight. I loved the aroma of crab, sweet and surprisingly complex, mixed with the many herbs and spices the contestants had included in their soups. I breathed in deeply, trying to predict what I was about to taste.

There was onion, garlic, paprika, and probably Texas's entire bay leaf supply. Over all of it was the fresh salty air of the Gulf of Mexico, which was only about one hundred yards away from the tent.

I inhaled again. Someone was going Asian since I could smell curry. That would be an interesting variation. I glanced down at the soup kettles and opened the lid of the one I thought was curry-based. It released a steamy cloud that smelled like my favorite Indian restaurant. I wafted it toward my face, part enjoyable odor, part steam bath. I couldn't wait to try that one.

"Here, smell this." I handed the lid to Daniel, then left to search for the competitor list.

I found the clipboard with the names of the contestants. "Let's see, we've got fifteen contestants: Sofia Delgado, Shanda Bennington,

Veronica Rossi, Isabella Rodriguez, Benjamin—" I stopped and groaned. "Great, Benjy Hayes is here."

"Benjy?" Daniel scowled. "As in your ex-boyfriend who was too stupid to realize what he had?"

"The one and only," a deep voice said behind me.

chapter two
· · ·

YOU'VE GOT *to be kidding me.* Two blasts from my cooking school past: my rival and my ex-boyfriend.

My stomach fluttered. "Hello, Benjy. I'm surprised to see you here." That was an understatement.

Daniel moved in front of me, drawing himself up to full height. Stepping around from behind him, I could see Benjy wasn't intimidated. I hadn't seen him in nine years, and he'd changed. He'd shaved off his blond hair—I suppose my nickname of Sandy wasn't accurate anymore—and sported a bald pate. It looked good on him. Some wrinkles fanned out from those blue eyes that had mesmerized me when I was young and naïve, but Benjy wore them well. He was still in top shape, with a thin waist and broad shoulders that stretched out his chef's whites, embroidered with Kimi's Kitchen, which must be the name of his restaurant.

"I live in Houston, less than an hour away, so I thought I'd come compete," he said, scrutinizing me. He didn't appear impressed. "You've lost weight."

Daniel stepped in front of me again. "She's been sick."

I moved next to my brother and nudged him with my hip. "That's a nice way to put it. Unfortunately, that's what happens when you decide to drink your calories rather than eat them. You don't look surprised by that information." I'd wondered if he had heard about my...situation. Although the gossip magazines had announced it to the world, Benjy never paid attention to the news or really anything that wasn't about food.

"I heard it from one of our former classmates," he admitted.

"Well, that person told the truth. I've been sober now, though, for four months, during which I've actually gained some of that weight back." Most women would have been appalled to gain ten pounds. I was glad. I still had about five more to gain before I was at a healthy weight.

He looked me up and down again, but not in a lecherous way. "You do look healthier than the last time I saw you on television."

"Thanks, I guess. You look different from the last time I saw you." I circled a finger around my head. "You had a heck of a lot more hair."

"I shaved it off for an event once. Decided it was easier to take care of. And customers couldn't claim my hair got in their food."

I laughed. "I get that. It's why I started doing a bun."

"Where's the husband? What was it, Simon something?"

Daniel made a noise of derision. Me, I was shocked Benjy knew anything about Simon. As I said, he never seemed to pay attention to gossip. Maybe he'd kept tabs on me. But why would he have done that? "Simon Levenson. And I don't know where he is. Probably huddled up somewhere with his lawyer, trying to figure out how to best get my money. Not that there's any to get."

"You're still wearing the ring."

I stared down at the gold band on my finger. A symbol of my mistakes. A symbol of trying to improve. "Well, I'm still legally married. And when I took my moral inventory for AA, one of the defects I identified in myself was that I never kept promises. It was why I wasn't able to quit drinking before, no matter who it hurt. I've resolved from now on to keep my promises. So until the state of California says I'm no longer married, I'm going to behave like I still am."

"Simon doesn't deserve it," Daniel said, then glanced at his ringing phone. His eyes widened. "Excuse me, I need to take this call."

He walked off, leaving Benjy and me alone. Well, alone with a hundred or so other people around. I was surprised my brother left me to fend for myself. Even though he was the younger brother, he'd always been protective of me, especially after my fall from grace. It must have been an important phone call.

Back in his systems administrator days, that would have meant that something had crashed catastrophically, and he'd be on his computer for hours trying to get the system up and running. But after my "crash," Daniel resigned from his job to help me. Now he was my business manager, not that I had much business to manage. Maybe he had found me another judging gig.

I looked back at Benjy, suddenly nervous. I normally don't have trouble talking—quite the opposite, I've always shared my thoughts, no matter how private or personal—but for some reason, I had no idea what to say to Benjy right now. After our breakup, we had barely spoken ten words to each other.

Inclining his head, Benjy asked, "So what's someone of your reputation doing here judging a tiny crab festival?"

Okay, here was a safe topic. "Considering my current reputation, I'm happy I'm not judging a bologna festival. I've fallen far. Gourmet Channel cancelled the show, the restaurant was losing money so badly that I had to close it, and people no longer trusted me. I barely have a pot to cook in."

Benjy smiled at my joke, but then his look turned serious. "I'm sorry to hear that happened to you."

I shrugged. "I did it to myself. So that's why I'm here. Trying to rebuild. I'm more curious why Heather's here."

"Oh, that's easy. She hates you. Anything she can do to make your life miserable, she's going to do it. Felt that way since culinary school. Why do you think she tried to go after me? I was yours, so she wanted me."

There it was. The topic I wanted to avoid. "According to the rumors, she succeeded."

He scowled. "I knew it. That's why you broke up with me."

"I didn't break up with you. You broke up with me."

"Semantics. You were about to dump me. I just beat you to it. I could see it in your eyes—you didn't believe I didn't sleep with

Heather, even though I told you I didn't. And I didn't." He pivoted on his Crocs and stormed off. I frowned at his back. He was lying. I knew he was.

Wasn't he?

I almost jumped ten feet when someone tapped me on the shoulder. Turning around, I saw Mayor Tom with a petite blonde. A blonde from a bottle, I thought, noticing the dark roots. I'd seen her earlier at the opening ceremony. Considering he'd kissed her while they were on stage, I assumed this was the wife he'd mentioned. Or things were more liberal here in Texas than I thought. She held out a hand.

"Good to see you again, Jackie," she said. Her grip was timid and weak. "Erica Wheeler," she said after a momentary hesitation, her voice matching the handshake. Even her outfit, a beige pantsuit with ecru high heels, was bland. The only spot of color was a delicate gold necklace with turquoise beads. Obviously, her husband was the more vivid and outgoing of the two.

"As I said, Erica is the third judge," Mayor Tom said. "She's—"

Greg Wright, the cameraman, was waving them over to the judging table.

"Oh, it's time for the tasting." Mayor Tom straightened his crab-patterned tie and gave a gentle shove to his wife. We walked toward the judging table, where Heather was already sitting on the far right.

I sat on the left, leaving the middle for the mayor's wife. I planned to stay as far away from Heather as possible.

The mayor brought over a tray with three bowls, placing one in front of each of us. We already had spoons, napkins, and a plastic bib, typically used while eating lobster. "Put that on," the mayor said.

"It's soup," I protested. "I've been able to eat without a bib for years. They stressed that at culinary school."

Mayor Tom laughed awkwardly. "It's just for the pictures."

The bib was white with bright red letters stating, *Get Crabby in Redding*. I sighed and tied the stupid thing around my neck. Mayor Tom started fluffing it a bit.

I grabbed his hand. "Mayor Tom, I usually insist on knowing someone at least a week before he reaches second base."

He blushed furiously. "I was making sure we could see the town name." Wisely, he turned his attention to his wife.

Greg moved the mayor out of the way and lifted his camera. "Okay, ready for pictures?"

"Quickly, please," Benjy said from the sidelines. "My soup is getting cold."

I was surprised they weren't conducting this taste test blind. It was their first year doing the competition, so they were bound to make mistakes. I'd definitely recommend that next year they not let the judges know who cooked which food. I would do my best not to be biased against my ex-boyfriend, but I couldn't guarantee the same for Heather, who also had a history with him. And Erica, being the mayor's wife, probably felt loyal to the local chefs.

"Don't rush art," Greg said, frowning. "Heather, do you mind switching with Erica? Again, I like the composition of blond, brown, blond."

Erica stood to swap seats without protest. Heather looked like she was going to complain but changed her mind and smiled. "Of course. I don't mind at all."

Greg shot a number of photos with us, switched lenses on the camera before attaching it to a tripod, and gestured at the mayor to start.

The mayor strode to the podium and began to speak into the microphone, addressing the audience. Being Friday evening, there weren't too many people in the crowd, maybe one hundred fifty or so. Tomorrow and Sunday should be more crowded, especially if the warm spring weather held out.

"Welcome to Redding Beach's First Annual Crab Festival. Tonight's contest will be the crab soup competition, and we'll have other competitions on Saturday and Sunday. All three contests will be judged by Gourmet Channel stars Heather Curtis and Jackie Norwood and, last but not least, my beautiful wife, Erica. Our first entry in the soup competition is Benjy Hayes, owner of Kimi's Kitchen located in Houston." The mayor stressed the city name, obviously happy that a big-city chef was competing in his small-town festival. "Benjy has named his soup 'Un-cream of Crab' because his recipe does not include dairy."

I groaned internally. Pandering much? I'm sure Heather would love this. I wasn't certain I would. What could replace the silky taste of cream? I took a deep breath, drawing in the aroma while I picked up my spoon. Smell was such an important aspect of the enjoyment and taste of food. People didn't take the time to appreciate the fragrance of food before shoveling it into their mouths. Benjy's soup was appropriately thick and creamy and smelled delectable. He'd gone for an East Coast-style crab soup, so I could smell the sweetness of the crab, the punch of garlic and spices—I guessed paprika, red pepper, and black pepper—as well as a slightly nutty odor. Was almond milk the dairy replacement? That could work, I mused, since it doesn't have a very overpowering taste.

Heather didn't bother enjoying the aromas and went straight to tasting. "It's so creamy," she said after the first spoonful, flirtatiously glancing at Benjy. She dipped her spoon again and raised it delicately to her lips. "To die for."

I didn't realize she meant that literally.

chapter three

. . .

I WAS POISED over my spoon, ready to take my own taste, when Heather inhaled sharply. She dropped the utensil, which clattered noisily onto the plastic table. Her face was flushed cherry-red and she was breathing rapidly. Not good. I dropped my own spoon and placed my hand on her back. "Are you allergic to crab?" That seemed like a ridiculous question since we were at a crab festival.

Heather turned to stare at me, her eyes unfocused.

"She's not!" a voice called from the audience. I looked out and saw Super Fan—Skylar—in the front row, standing. "In the December sixth episode of *The Clean Cook*, she said she loves crab, but she never cooks with it on her show because it's a common allergen. I don't think she has any allergies herself."

Just then, Heather's eyes rolled back and she started convulsing. She might not be allergic, but this was really, really not good. I grabbed her shoulders as she slid out of the chair—wow, she weighed more than I thought. Thankfully, Mayor Tom rushed over and helped me ease her down to the ground. I tried to cradle her head with my free arm.

I heard Erica yelling for someone to call 9-1-1 and run to the medical tent, but I was scanning my memory for my basic first-aid training. When her jerking motion stopped, I rolled her onto her side into the recovery position, which was recommended when someone was experiencing a seizure.

Most chefs know basic first aid so they can help if a guest chokes on food. It was bad for business when customers died in your restaurant. But I had no freaking idea what to do now. Where were the EMTs?

I saw Benjy leaning over the edge of the table, his skin pale and his blue eyes wide as he stared at the scene. Was he worried about Heather…or about the fact she'd been eating his soup?

Finally, the EMTs arrived, so I moved aside from where I'd been kneeling next to Heather. I'd never been so happy to let professionals take over. As I stood, I smelled a whiff of almonds. It must have been the almond milk, but it smelled bitter. Did Benjy burn the soup?

One of the EMTs pulled me aside. "Can you tell me what happened?"

"I don't know," I answered honestly. "She ate a couple spoonfuls of soup, then suddenly turned bright red and started gasping for air. Then she went into convulsions. She's not allergic to crab," I rushed to say, "at least according to one of her fans who said Heather had no allergies."

"Who made the soup?"

I motioned Benjy over. "This is the chef who made the soup she was eating."

"What was in the soup?" the EMT demanded.

Benjy dragged his eyes away from the horrible scene unfolding and blinked. "Um, crab. Shallots and garlic. Tapioca starch, paprika, black pepper, salt, almond butter, and almond milk."

I'd been right about the cream replacement.

The EMT returned to assist their fellow workers as Heather was placed on a gurney.

As I stood awkwardly next to Benjy, I searched the crowd for my brother. Where was he? Normally, he'd have been by my side, making sure I was okay.

Two uniformed police officers entered the tent, arrowing straight for the EMT who'd questioned me.

"Why did you cater to Heather?" I whispered to Benjy. I immediately regretted the question. Once again, I blurted whatever was in my mind, not thinking how it would sound.

"Why did I what?"

"Cater to her." I could have kicked myself for starting this conversation, but I couldn't drop it now. "With the *Un-cream of Crab*. Going dairy free and all that?"

He shook his head quickly like my question was an annoying gnat buzzing around. "It's what I do already at *Kimi's Kitchen*. All our dishes are dairy free."

"Really? I don't remember you being interested in that at culinary school."

He shifted his gaze toward me and gently guided my shoulder, ensuring I faced him while the EMTs carted Heather away. It appeared he wished to shield me from witnessing the scene. "I wasn't interested in allergy-free food until Kimi."

I had wondered about the name of his restaurant, thinking Kimi might be his wife. He wasn't wearing a wedding band, but plenty of chefs don't.

"Kimi is my niece."

Kimi was his niece, not his wife. That was good to hear. Wait. I shouldn't care whether Benjy had a wife or not. He'd cheated on me. Not to mention, I was in recovery and shouldn't be thinking about romantic entanglements. Still, I vaguely remembered him talking about his sister's pregnancy when we were dating. How sweet that he named his restaurant after his niece.

"When she was four years old, she was diagnosed with lymphoma," he continued. "They caught it early and treated it aggressively, chemo and radiation and all that. It worked. She's been in remission for five years. But we believe the treatments gave her severe food allergies she hadn't had before the cancer." He shrugged. "We're just happy she's alive, of course, but it does make her life and my sister's life difficult. I decided to figure out how to make dairy-free food tasty, and it turned into the theme of my restaurant."

Okay, I felt like a jerk.

He looked me directly in the eyes. "If I did any pandering in this recipe, it's that I eliminated an ingredient. Typically, I use sherry to enhance the flavor. For your sake, I left it out. The mayor should have made that one of the stipulations of the contest."

Now I felt like a double jerk times a hundred.

"I'm sorry, Benjy. And thank you." I looked away and noticed police officers were now talking to the mayor. "I'm sorry for thinking you were catering to Heather. And sorry about your niece, although I'm glad she's in remission." I realized something. "Is that why you shaved off your hair?"

He nodded. "Kimi was devastated when she lost her hair. When she saw me bald, she giggled. It was the first time I'd heard her laugh in months." He smiled, then his eyes widened. I turned to see two uniformed police officers, one short, one tall, homing in on us.

The taller one spoke. "Ms. Norwood, we understand you were seated beside Ms. Curtis when she collapsed. We'd like to talk to you about that. And, Mr. Hayes, we'd like to talk to you about your soup."

Officer Short guided me in one direction, and Officer Tall led Benjy in another. We glanced at each other before separating. I noticed someone had herded the contestants and audience members to the other side of the tent. Skylar was among them. Surprisingly, she didn't appear that upset. She just stood there with a blank expression. Poor thing was probably in shock.

The mayor and his wife were talking to another police officer, and finally, I saw my brother running into the tent. He still had his cell phone in one hand and a look of concern on his face. I waved to catch his attention and show him I wasn't the one in the ambulance. I considered signaling it was Heather who was ill, but A: I didn't want to draw attention to myself and B: though I'm good at charades, that went beyond my abilities. I was sure he'd hear from the others in the tent anyway.

The officer gestured to a folding chair. "Sit, please."

I obediently did as he said because I didn't want to do anything to annoy the law. During my tumultuous alcoholic phase, I found myself entangled with the police. While I'd been smart enough to *never* drive while intoxicated, I did have a drunk and disorderly or two. So let's just say the police made me nervous.

Looming over me, he introduced himself. "Ms. Norwood, I'm Officer Short."

No way! His name really *was* Officer Short. I'd always had a propensity to nickname people before I learned their real names, but this was the first time I'd nailed it. I turned my laugh into a cough, hoping he took it for nerves.

He frowned, then sat in a chair across from me. "I have a few questions to ask about what happened prior to Ms. Curtis's collapse."

I recounted the events from when I'd sat at the judging table.

"How about before that?" he asked, not looking up from where he was writing in a notebook.

"Before that? Like, how long before?"

He glanced up and gave me a serious glare from beady brown eyes. "Let's take the last two hours."

"Okay." I paused while giving that some thought. "Well, I suppose two hours earlier, I was probably leaving my hotel."

"Which is?"

His interruption while I tried to concentrate annoyed me. "I'm at the Redding Beach Hotel. Room 233."

He raised an eyebrow. "A celebrity like you, at that place? It doesn't even have room service. Or a bar." Considering the emphasis on that last word, he'd heard of me and my recent troubles.

I clenched my hands under the table and fought not to make a snide comment. "The town is paying for my room, and that is where they selected."

"So you left the hotel. How?"

"I walked." I waved a hand in the direction of the hotel. "It's not too far, and it's a nice day. My brother Daniel and I walked here."

"Did you make any stops?"

"No." Why was he asking me so many questions about my actions?

"What did you do when you arrived?"

"Went to the restroom." I badly wanted to give him graphic details on what happened there. "Watched the end of the opening ceremony—we were a little late—and then wandered around the tent for the VIP party. Met Heather Curtis."

"For the first time?"

"Definitely not for the first time." How much information should I give? I should probably leave out the fact we hated each other. "I've known her for over ten years, since we went to culinary school together. I often saw her at Gourmet Channel events. But I haven't seen her since last October."

"Did you have an altercation with her today?"

"An altercation?" Crap. The mayor must have told him about that. "I wouldn't call it that. She came over to me and said a few snotty things, which I tried not to react to. Then the mayor came over and broke the news that she was also a celebrity judge here."

He scribbled furiously in the notebook. "You didn't know that before today?"

"I didn't know that until about an hour ago. Why are you asking these questions?"

Officer Short puffed up his chest but didn't respond. I'm not psychic, but I swear I could see "I'll ask the questions here" in big letters above his head. "What did you do after that?"

"I walked back to where my brother was sitting." I pointed for clarification. "We talked a little, then he asked how many competitors there were. I didn't know, so we headed to the food-prep area."

"You were in this food-prep area? Who else was there?"

I closed my eyes, trying to picture it. "I don't remember, exactly. A couple of chefs, maybe three, were there doing last-minute preparation. One had bright-orange hair. I can tell you what herbs they were chopping if that would help."

"Did you touch any of the soups in any way?"

I stiffened at that question. "What? Of course not. I'd never interfere with another chef's food. Especially not during a competition."

"How about your brother? Did he touch anything?"

"Absolutely not."

He scribbled in his notebook. "What did you do next?"

"I talked to Benjamin Hayes." I prayed he wouldn't ask the specifics about that conversation. "Then it was time for the competition, so I sat down at the judging table."

"Have you been drinking today?" He gave me what must be his bad-cop stare.

Somehow, I doubted Benjy was being asked this question. "Not since January."

He seemed ready to ask another question when the phone at his hip buzzed. He checked the screen, then slowly raised his gaze.

His expression made me uneasy.

"That was the hospital."

His tone also made me uneasy. This wasn't good.

"Heather Curtis is dead."

chapter four
. . .

THE SOUND of the ocean roaring filled my ears as I stared at Officer Short. I actually glanced over at the gulf to make certain there wasn't a tidal wave coming. It took a few seconds to realize that was just the sound of my pulse racing after hearing the news.

How could she be dead? I'd just seen her. She'd been sitting beside me, antagonizing me as always. And now, dead?

I took a few deep breaths, aware that Officer Short was watching me, and not in a concerned, worried manner, but in a deeply suspicious one. Did he think someone had done something to cause this death? Did he think *I* had anything to do with it?

Once I had control of myself again, I asked the obvious question. "Do they know why? She's young and looks healthy enough." I realized I'd said looks as if she were still with us.

Officer Short firmed his lips. "I am not at liberty to discuss that."

"She has family." I struggled to remember details from our graduation. "Her parents, a sister. Have they been informed?"

"We are in the process of handling that. I must ask that you not contact them or anyone else, including the media, regarding this incident."

"Of course." I had no way of contacting her family, and I actively avoided the media these days.

"You'll remain in town?"

"As far as I know," I said. "The plan was to stay until Tuesday, but if the festival is cancelled, I don't know if Mayor Tom will want to pay for my hotel room." I pondered on that possibility. I supposed if I had to, I could share Daniel's room with its two queen beds. It would be awkward. I hadn't shared a room with Daniel since he was a baby.

"Please contact us if you have anything additional we should know." Officer Short handed me a card in dismissal.

I stood, wondering if he would say that cliché about not leaving town. They always said it on those cop shows. Or was that just television?

When he didn't say anything further, I shoved the card in my purse and turned around.

"And Ms. Norwood," Officer Short said to my back. "Don't leave town."

I guessed they did say it.

I booked it out of there before he could add or ask anything else. Glancing past the crowd, I saw Benjy still talking to the tall officer. I wondered if he'd been told about Heather's death yet. I worried about him. We'd dated for over a year before the breakup, and we had been friends before that, so during that time, I'd known him well. He was always good at assuming responsibility for his actions but often went too far, taking the blame for things that weren't his fault. If something in his soup had led to Heather's death, the Benjy I used to know would be wracked by guilt forever.

I scanned the area, searching for Daniel. I found him right outside the tent, waving at me. I jogged over as fast as my flip-flops would allow.

"What happened?" Daniel asked. "I heard one of the judges was sick. Is that true? Why are the police here? Why'd they need to talk to you? What—"

I held up a hand to cut him off. "I need a drink before I tell you," I said. Daniel frowned. "No, not that type. I'm just parched. I need some water." I placed a hand on my stomach when it growled. "And some food. I'm starving." As I usually did before a tasting, I hadn't eaten anything.

"You didn't get to eat anything?" Daniel furrowed his brow. "Now I really want to know what happened."

We grabbed some fried food from a boardwalk restaurant and sat at a picnic table. There weren't many people around, so it was easy to find a semi-private area to talk.

"So, what's up?" Daniel asked, picking up a french fry.

The fry remained uneaten as I spilled the whole story. "The officer told me she passed away. I can't believe it," I said, shaking my head. "And I have no idea what happened. She couldn't have been allergic to crab. She wasn't stupid. No way would she have been judging a crab festival with a shellfish allergy."

Daniel had an odd look on his face. "What color did you say her face was?"

"Red."

"How red? Like, would you say cherry-red?"

"I don't know. It all happened so fast." Reluctantly, I pictured her face during the last moments of her life. "Yes, I suppose that would be accurate. At least at first, then it turned even darker red."

"It sounds like cyanide poisoning."

"Get out." I raised an eyebrow. "You have been reading way too many mysteries, little brother."

"I haven't just been reading mysteries, I've been…never mind. My point is that after reading these mysteries, I've done research. And the way you just described it sounds like cyanide poisoning to me." He pulled out his cell phone and poked at the screen.

"Seriously, too many Agatha Christie novels," I rolled my eyes. "Daniel, ever since you were a kid, you've found mysteries. Remember the Mystery of the Stolen Car? You interrogated everyone in the neighborhood when the Ford next door disappeared."

Daniel glanced up from his phone, scowling. "Well, how was I to know it was at the mechanic? I was seven!"

"Fine. How about when you thought your high-school best friend was selling drugs?"

"He was acting suspiciously. And he was hiding something."

I threw my hands in the air. "He was planning your surprise birthday party!"

"Like I said. He was hiding something. Anyway, look!" He thrust his phone at me.

I glanced at the website on his screen. "Oh. Wikipedia. That's reliable. You know people can write whatever they want."

Now Daniel rolled his eyes. "This isn't a college essay, Jackie. I don't need three primary sources. Just read it."

"Fine." The more I read, the more concerned I got. "Seizures. Check. Rapid breathing. Check. Cherry-red skin color and a bitter almond smell." I met Daniel's eyes over his phone. "Check."

"So you agree?" Daniel said.

"Maybe, but who the hell would poison Heather?"

"That's what we'd like to know," said a familiar male voice behind me.

"Hello, Officer Short." As I turned to face him, I noticed another man with him, this one older and taller—not difficult to do the latter—in khakis and a white polo that contrasted with his dark skin. I stood. "Daniel, this is Officer Short and …?"

"Detective Lloyd Preston," the khakied man said. "Ms. Norwood, in light of new information, we'd like to talk to you again."

"And I'd like to talk to you, Mr. Norwood." Officer Short fingered his handcuffs as he glared at my brother. I presumed he was trying to appear threatening and imposing, considering he was almost a foot shorter than Daniel, but it looked like he was fidgeting.

"Daniel wasn't there when it happened," I protested.

Officer Short raised an eyebrow. "Yes, we noticed that. Funny that he was in the vicinity earlier but then disappeared before—"

"Officer," Detective Preston said sternly. "That's enough. Ms. Norwood, if you would come with me." Daniel and I dumped our sadly uneaten food and followed the detective and police officer back to the festival grounds. Daniel and Officer Short went to the tent where we'd been earlier, and Detective Preston led me to another tent. This one appeared to be commandeered from one of the craft vendors. I saw some pretty blouses, but this wasn't the time to window shop. Preston pointed to a chair next to a narrow folding table. I took the offered seat, eager to seem accommodating.

"I have Officer Short's notes." He shuffled the papers in front of him. "But could you please go over what happened, starting from when you arrived at the festival?"

I repeated my story about the trinity of crappy discoveries. First, Heather being here, in Texas. Then the fact we were co-judges. And then, finally, that my ex-boyfriend was here. I figured honesty was the best policy when dealing with the police. I choked up slightly when I relayed the scene with Heather, knowing this time that she had died. "Then, after speaking to Officer Short, I met up with Daniel."

"Is that unusual?"

"Speaking to Officer Short? Yes, I try to avoid the police."

When he frowned, I realized being a smart aleck wasn't the best policy. "I'm sorry. Do you mean meeting up with Daniel?"

"I would have thought, with how important you said this festival is to restart your career, that he would have been in the audience," Preston said.

I had to agree, but I didn't think it was a good idea to admit that. "He got a phone call right before the start of the first tasting." I frowned. In my haste to tell him about Heather, I hadn't asked about the phone call.

Preston nodded, scribbling something in a notebook. "And when you met, you decided to look up information on poison?"

"No. First, we decided to eat dinner since I fasted today in preparation for the tasting tonight." My stomach grumbled, reminding me I'd never had the chance to eat my fried shrimp. "Then, when I told Daniel what happened and how Heather convulsed, he thought it might be cyanide poisoning."

"Seems like a quick and specific leap of logic there," Preston said.

"Honestly, that's typical behavior for Daniel. Both of us have a lack of impulse control. His, fortunately, presents itself as impulsive thoughts rather than the destructive behavior that is my downfall." Like I said, I was going to be honest with the police. "I have to admit, once we looked up symptoms, they seemed to fit. The soup had a slight almond smell, both in the bowl, but even more, when she had already started convulsing, it smelled like burnt almonds. Daniel, who loves mysteries, remembered that cyanide is supposed to smell like bitter almond."

"And you think someone put cyanide in Ms. Curtis' soup?" the detective asked. I admired his ability to sound casual.

"I doubt it would end up there accidentally, so yes? I mean, *if* it was cyanide."

"Who do you think would have reason to do that? Would anyone want to kill her?"

Was he asking me if *I* wanted to kill her? They'd already heard from the mayor about the animosity between Heather and me. If I didn't admit to disliking her, would I look guilty? Not that I hated her so much I'd want to kill her. Maybe I should just…

I was suddenly aware that I was taking far too long to answer the question. I raised my eyes and noticed Detective Preston watching me, once again revealing nothing in his gaze.

I sighed. "I wouldn't say that I ever wanted to *kill* her. But we've never gotten along since we were in culinary school together about ten years ago. I'd even have called us adversaries, although most of the hostility came from her side because she was jealous of my success."

"But you haven't had much success lately, have you?"

I stared down at the tent floor, listening to the waves. "I haven't, but I have myself to blame for that. Heather had no part in ruining my life. I did it all on my own." I looked up now, directly into the detective's dark-brown eyes. "I didn't like Heather, but I wouldn't kill her. She was a pain, often petty, but she wasn't so meaningful in my life that I'd do something like that."

"Would Mr. Hayes?"

"Benjy?" I shook my head so hard it gave me a slight headache. "No way. Benjy wouldn't hurt a fly."

"But he had a history with her as well, correct?" He set down his pen and read his notes. "According to him, she was the reason you and he broke up in culinary school."

I closed my eyes. Benjy was also too honest for his own good. "Yes, that's true. There were rumors he was cheating on me with Heather."

"Were they true?"

"I thought so at the time," I admitted. "Now...I'm not so sure. Honestly, at the time, I didn't even give Benjy a chance. I just took Heather's claims for granted."

"And now you know that it didn't happen? Some people would get pretty upset at that. Even murderously upset."

"Those people need to take anger management courses," I said. "Like I said, I disliked Heather, and realizing that she manipulated me pissed me off, but not enough to want her dead. Well, maybe enough to want her dead, but not enough to… actively make her dead."

"So again, who do you know would want that enough?" He picked up his pen.

I considered it. I wouldn't be so conceited to think losing me was enough to make Benjy kill her. There were other people at culinary school who'd hated her too, but again, worth killing for? "I can't think of anyone. But honestly, I don't know much about her personal life."

He angled his head. "Really?"

"Really."

He nodded slowly. "Well, if you think of someone or something else, please let me know." Like Officer Short, Detective Preston handed me a card.

I took a few steps away, glad to be done with the second interrogation when I did actually think of something else. "Wait a minute!" I went back and sat down again.

He raised an eyebrow.

"If there was poison," I said to him. "It wasn't meant for Heather."

chapter five
. . .

"WHAT MAKES YOU SAY THAT?" Detective Preston asked, eyebrows raised.

"Because it wasn't supposed to be her bowl!" How could I have forgotten this when I first described how the tasting went? "The mayor was the one who placed the bowls. But then Greg—the cameraman—made us switch seats."

"Why did he do that?"

I shrugged. "He has some weird thing where he likes to arrange people by hair color. So he put the blondes at either end and Heather in the middle. So the poisoned bowl was meant for Erica."

Finally, I saw the detective react as his eyes widened. He then returned to that blank look that cops must practice. "A reminder that we haven't determined whether there even was poison," Detective Preston said.

"I guess the question would then be," I said, "who would want to kill Erica? I don't know her. But I suppose the husband would be the first suspect, wouldn't he? Especially because he was the one who set the bowls down."

Detective Preston clenched his jaw. "Ms. Norwood, I'd ask you to please keep this fact and theory to yourself for now. No one should be jumping to conclusions about anything."

"But you asked me who was trying to kill Heather."

He put his blank face on again. "No, I never said that either. You were theorizing that someone tried to. I merely asked you who would have wanted to kill her. But we do appreciate your cooperation, and again, please keep this information to yourself."

I nodded but didn't promise.

I texted Daniel as I walked out of the tent, hoping he was already done with his interview with Officer Short.

The competition area was fairly deserted at this point. It was late, so the festival was finished for the evening anyway, even without the death and subsequent investigation. I wondered what they would do with the festival now. Would they cancel it now that there was a death?

"You have to cancel the festival!"

I glanced around, confused. Was someone reading my thoughts?

"Are you kidding? After I worked so hard to arrange everything?"

I recognized the mayor's voice. I saw him sitting on a nearby bench, facing away from me. Erica sat next to him. There were some overhead lights in the area, illuminating them both. Even though I was in a dark area, I didn't want them to notice me. Spotting a nearby food booth, I ducked behind it.

"Someone died, Tom. Don't you think it's disrespectful to still hold the festival?"

"I'm sure Heather would have wanted us to continue on."

I wasn't so sure about that, actually. Heather never wanted anything that didn't benefit Heather. The success or lack of success wouldn't matter to her. Especially now, being dead and all.

"Maybe we could name one of the contests after her," the mayor continued. "The Heather Curtis Crab Cake Contest sounds pretty good."

"Wait. You still intend to go forward with the cooking contests?"

Erica's voice was filled with shock and disbelief. I couldn't blame her. "The police, no matter how much they keep playing off that this is all hypothetical, think the soup was poisoned, and you want me to keep tasting food?"

"I'm sure her death was just a mistake."

Well, yes, I thought, if Erica was the intended victim.

"And do you think anyone is going to want to eat *any* of the food that's available at this festival after someone died from a 'mistake?'" I couldn't see Erica, but I imagined her making air quotes around "mistake."

The mayor took a minute to answer. "I'm sure everyone will be fine eating the whole crab. And we've got to sell those. We bought tons of them. Literally."

Erica sighed. "I suspect the vendors selling soups won't be terribly popular." I could hear tapping. It sounded like she was drumming her fingernails on the bench. "You really want to have the contests too? Who are you going to get as a third judge, assuming Jackie stays?"

"Can't we just stick to two judges?"

That wouldn't work, I knew. You needed an odd number to avoid ties. I smiled when Erica said the same thing.

"And who else do you think is willing to risk their life for this stupid festival?"

"I'll find someone. And it's not a stupid festival. The success of this festival could make or break this town. Could make or break my career."

"And it always comes down to your career," Erica said quietly. I heard some rustling, then the sound of footsteps. Taking a chance, I peeked around and saw her walking away, staring down at the ground. The mayor was still on the bench, both arms spread out on the back rest. When I saw someone else approaching, I ducked back behind the booth.

"Good evening, Mayor." Detective Preston. "Do you have a moment?"

"Of course, I always have a moment for the boys in blue. Have you had any luck in finding out what killed our celebrity guest?"

"We are still waiting to get back the analysis on the soup. But assuming it is poisoned, we have reason to believe Ms. Curtis wasn't the intended victim."

I listened closely as the detective ran through the hypothesis—my hypothesis, thank you very much—that the soup might not have been intended for Heather.

"You believe someone tried to kill my wife!" The mayor was really shocked, or, if it was true to always look at the spouse, then he was a phenomenal actor.

"It's a possibility," the detective hedged.

Silence stretched out. I suspected Detective Preston was using it as a weapon. The mayor gasped.

"You think *I* did it?"

Oh, how I longed for a glimpse of the mayor's face at that moment.

"I didn't say that," the detective said calmly.

"But you think it's possible," said the mayor. "Why would I want to kill my wife? And more importantly, why would I do that at *my* festival?"

I frowned. More importantly? The mayor sounded more protective of his festival than of his wife. But he had a point. The mayor was obviously invested in this festival. Someone dying—whether it was his wife or his celebrity judge—could negatively impact the festival's success.

Again, the detective stayed silent.

"You know," the mayor said. "I have plenty of enemies, those who opposed me when I was running for mayor, that might go after Erica to get at me. Why don't you check their alibis or whatever?"

"We're still exploring many angles, Mayor Wheeler. If you have any leads on people who might have motives, we'd appreciate them."

"Well, I'm not certain I feel comfortable giving names. Wouldn't want to expose myself to a defamation suit."

I rolled my eyes. What a way to throw suspicion away from yourself without actually naming anyone.

"Of course, sir. We'll be discreet with any names you provide."

"I'll get back to you. In the meantime, I need to prepare for tomorrow."

"You're not cancelling the festival?" Detective Preston asked.

"You sound like my wife," the mayor complained. "First of all, we don't actually know that Heather died from poison."

"The EMT felt strongly that the symptoms indicated cyanide."

"Still, it's not confirmed. And we, by that I meant the people of Redding Beach, have a lot riding on the success of this festival. Everyone would be impacted if we cancelled it. The hotels, the restaurants, the shops."

"And if someone else dies?"

"No one else will. I'm sure this was a one-time thing." I could hear rapid footsteps, which I assumed were the mayor's.

"I hope he's right," Detective Preston said to himself.

I waited until his footsteps also faded, then I escaped from my hiding place and jogged away. I jumped when I got a text, thankful it hadn't arrived while I was eavesdropping.

Checking my phone, I saw Daniel had finished his interview with Officer Short and was ready to return to the hotel.

"Can we please grab something to eat?" I asked when we met up. "I still haven't eaten today."

Since everything else seemed closed, my highbrow culinary taste buds were forced to settle for a hot dog at a local convenience store. As hungry as I was, it hit the spot. "As good as filet mignon," I said around a bite of the mystery meat.

After sating my appetite, we walked back to our hotel room. I asked Daniel about his interview, then filled him in on mine with Detective Preston and what I had overheard. "I'm not sure if Detective Preston suspects the mayor, but I do."

"Why would the mayor want to kill his wife?" Daniel asked.

"You haven't been married, Daniel. Trust me, there are many times you might want to kill your spouse." God knows I'd thought about it.

"You only think that because you had a bad marriage, Jackie, and before you say it, it's not just because of your drinking. Nor did we get a very good example from Mom and Dad. But most marriages are better. They have to be, or no one would want to get married."

I couldn't counter that argument.

Daniel stopped outside our hotel and turned to face me. "But my real question would be, why would the mayor want to kill his wife right then and there? Not only because it would negatively affect the festival he's obviously invested in, but also because by committing murder in such a public fashion, the police would investigate more thoroughly than, say, an accident at home."

"Still..." I couldn't counter that argument either. I hated when Daniel was right, especially when some of his ideas were crazy. "Well, who else would want to kill Erica?"

Daniel shrugged and opened up the glass doors to the lobby. "That's up to the police to find out."

I snorted. "Detective Preston, maybe. But Officer Short? He doesn't seem too good at his job." I looked up and saw Officer Short at the front desk, glaring in my direction. Crap.

chapter six
...

I HELD MY BREATH, waiting for Officer Short to whip out his handcuffs. Thankfully, he just glared for a few more seconds, then returned to his conversation with the front desk clerk.

I said good night to Daniel as we separated into our adjoining rooms, shut the door behind me, and leaned against the door. I quickly glanced around my small room, hoping to find something to take my mind off Heather's death. I've heard it said that everything is bigger in Texas, but the reality here was quite the opposite. The room was so cramped that it could barely fit a double bed. Not that it mattered. I was sleeping alone anyway. I briefly thought about my soon-to-be-ex and wondered if he was in a similar situation or if he had already moved on to someone new.

I sunk onto the bed, wincing as overused springs poked at my lower back. I longed for the days of five-star hotels and luxury goods.

Not that I had grown up rich. Far from that. My parents had drunk away any money they managed to make. I learned to cook at an early age out of necessity, desperate to feed Daniel and myself from whatever ingredients we had on hand. It was why I'd done so well in the cooking competitions, whipping up a delicious meal from a basket full of unusual and unrelated items. That was called dinner in my house.

Then as an adult, I became the alcoholic offspring who, sadly, sought solace in alcohol as well. A walking cautionary tale. I know it was wrong, but a drink sure sounded good right now.

Fortunately, my phone rang, distracting me from temptation. I got up to retrieve it from my purse, saw the readout, and was instantly relieved. My sponsor had a sixth sense for this.

"Hello, April. How did you know? Spidey sense going off that I wanted a drink?"

"No, Jacqueline." April always spoke proper English with the slightest accent from her birthplace in Taiwan. "I am watching the news, and I thought it prudent to check on you."

I sat on the edge of the bed, tracing the pattern on the faded bedspread. "I'm okay. I mean, I'm upset, but as you know, Heather wasn't actually my friend."

She made a noise somewhere between a tsk and a harumph. "That is an understatement. In fact, it surprises me you accepted this assignment, knowing Heather would be there. I keep telling you, you can come cook in one of my places."

April owned *Little Dragon*, an empire of upscale Chinese restaurants in San Francisco's Chinatown. She'd offered me a number of positions: chef de cuisine, sous chef, purchasing manager.

"As always, I appreciate the offer, I do. But I'm trying to prove to myself that I can make it on my own two feet. So that means taking gigs like this. Even when they surprise me with someone like Heather."

"You mean you were unaware she would be there? I bet that woman just rubbed it in your face."

I sighed. "She did, but I'm trying not to speak ill of the dead."

"Why not?" she responded sharply. "There is a saying in Chinese that translated means, 'Even death is not enough to compensate for your sins.' She is not a saint now that she is deceased. And it does not make you a bad person if you still have negative thoughts about her."

I turned and stretched out on the bed. "I suppose you're right. I do feel bad that a life has been lost. I feel sorry for her mother and father…and a younger sister, I believe. But other than that…"

"That is to be understood. She was a stick in your side. A total—"

"Thorn in your side," I corrected, smiling.

"No, thorns are small and slightly annoying. A stick is big and antagonizing. She was a stick. I also met this woman. She once came to my restaurant and was a complete prima donna, making outlandish demands upon my staff."

I sat upright. "Did she mention any allergies?"

"I do not recall. But I can check right now. We keep files on our VIPs, especially those overly demanding, which often seems to correlate." I heard her pecking away at a keyboard. "No. She has no allergies listed."

That confirmed what Skylar had said.

"Although she requested no mushrooms," April continued, "it is listed as a personal preference, not an allergy. And she does not like spicy food, said it gave her indigestion. Why she would choose to come to a Sichuan restaurant, I do not understand."

"What did she order?"

As expected, April had that information ready. "Lobster with ginger and scallions."

Well, that pretty much ruled out a shellfish allergy. When April snorted, I raised my eyebrows. "What?"

"Her date had sweet and sour pork. I understand some people do prefer the more Americanized versions of Chinese food. But again, why come to an upscale Chinese restaurant if you are going to order sweet and sour pork?"

"That would be like going to a fancy steakhouse and ordering a hamburger." I wondered who her date was. It didn't sound like someone with a discerning palate. I couldn't talk. I had married Simon, who didn't have sophisticated taste.

"But you are doing okay? No cravings?"

"Oh, there are cravings," I said. "But I'm resisting. I didn't like myself when I drank. I'm trying to become someone I like again."

"That is an admirable goal. You know how it works: call me if you need help, okay?"

"I will, April. Thank you for checking on me. Talk to you later." I hung up, then turned on the television to hear what the news had to say.

After finding the local news, I caught them just before going to a commercial break with the teaser, *"Upcoming: Death at the Redding Beach crab festival."* I bounced my knees as I waited through endless commercials.

The newscaster, a young and beautiful Hispanic woman, first talked about tomorrow's weather—eighty degrees but rainy—before getting to the big story. "A shocking start to today's opening night at the Redding Beach crab festival. Heather Curtis, Gourmet Channel's current darling and star of *The Clean Cook*, collapsed after sampling some crab soup. She later passed away at the nearby Hamilton Medical Center. Police are investigating the cause of death. Neither of the other two judges was affected."

I was miffed they didn't mention my name. Not that I wanted to be associated with a food-related death, but any publicity was good publicity, right?

"Benjy Hayes, executive chef of Houston-based Kimi's Kitchen, prepared the soup that was Heather's last meal. He was unable to be reached for comment. Prior to owning his own restaurant, which opened three years ago, Mr. Hayes was sous chef at Taurus, also in Houston, that closed during an E. coli outbreak which affected several restaurants in the area."

Okay, maybe there is bad publicity. Poor Benjy. Food safety was always a concern for any restaurateur. I remembered when that outbreak happened. I hadn't realized he'd been affected. Could E. coli have been the culprit here as well? No, I hadn't heard of E. coli causing the symptoms Heather had exhibited. And it didn't normally kill someone young and healthy. At least, I assumed Heather was healthy.

The internet would tell all.

The press didn't seem to believe in privacy for public figures, medical or otherwise. I opened my computer and typed Heather's name into the search bar.

An hour later, I was sick of article after article about how Clean Cooking had changed her life. How it cured her prediabetes, cleared up her skin, and improved her acid reflux.

Nothing that would indicate why a bowl of soup would cause her to die. Not a word about her own personal allergies. The woman's highly-rated television show was entirely devoted to eliminating common allergens, yet not one article, blog post, or interview pointed to Heather having allergies herself. And I watched the episode of *The Clean Cook* Skylar mentioned. Heather had clearly indicated she loved crab.

What if Daniel was right about the cyanide, and it had been murder? But a murder intended for Erica, and Heather just was in the wrong place at the wrong time.

I switched my search. Time to stalk the mayor. An easy task, I found out quickly. He was all over social media. Facebook, Twitter, Instagram, Snapchat, TikTok, if there was a platform, he was on it. And posting everywhere, especially in the weeks leading up to the festival.

His Facebook profile was completely public, so I learned he graduated from Rice University with dual majors in Political Science and Criminal Justice. Interesting. He was a fan of the Houston Texans, Houston Astros, and the Houston Rockets. I'm sure if there had been a Houston hockey team, he would have been all over that too.

He had been the mayor of Redding Beach for two years, with much of his campaign platform focused on bringing tourism to the area. While she was in some photos, he seldom mentioned Erica, other than one post last year about their five-year anniversary. Evidently, wood was the traditional gift, so he had purchased a cutting board for her with Redding Beach etched into it.

Out of curiosity, I took a peek at Erica's Facebook profile. Nothing much to learn there due to her strict privacy settings. She was listed as Erica Wheeler, no maiden name. I shrugged. Although most of my friends had both listed in their profile—to make it easier to be found by high school or college friends—some of them just had their married names. And some, like me, hadn't changed their last name at all. I'd already been established in my career as Jackie Norwood by the time I married Simon.

There were a couple of pictures posted of Erica and Mayor Tom at events, but other than that, all of her information was private for friends only. I went ahead and hit the Add Friend button. How could we not be friends after what we had gone through together?

I kept searching.

Heather's fan, Skylar Brooks, was not on Facebook. I knew the younger generations abandoned Facebook once their parents and even grandparents joined it, but a quick look at the trendier platforms didn't yield any results either.

Hesitating, I looked up Benjy, something I had resisted until today. Of course, being in the same industry, I'd seen his name pop up now and again, but I deliberately avoided keeping tabs on him. I was impressed with what I read. Other than the E. coli outbreak, which happened before he was head chef, the reviews were overwhelmingly positive. He'd also had great success in competitive cooking shows, both locally and nationally, although he tended to stick to shows on that *other* food-themed network. Although he had competed and won on *Hacked*, a few months after Heather and I competed.

I leaned back in my chair. I didn't think Benjy would have tried to kill Heather. I shook my head, remembering the soup hadn't been meant for Heather. It'd been meant for Erica. Unless the cameraman had been in on it. I shook my head again, trying to align my scattered thoughts.

I was glad I wasn't Detective Preston. It was hard enough to find a killer. I'm sure it was even harder to find one when you didn't know who the intended victim was.

chapter seven
. . .

THIS WAS A BAD IDEA. *No. It was a good idea.*

During rehab, I'd started running each morning. It was healthy, gave me a reason to get up in the morning, and the endorphins it produced felt better than anything I had managed to get from alcohol. At least, I told myself that. Plus, it let me practice my commitment skills, which had rusted while drinking.

Getting started was harder this morning. The alarm clock said it was seven, but my body, still on Pacific time, thought it was five.

Reluctantly, I threw on some blue running tights, a tank top that said, "Needs Salt," and my running shoes. After pulling my hair back into a high ponytail, I added a ball cap and went downstairs.

Stepping into the warm, humid air, I thought briefly of skipping the run in lieu of a swim in the cooler waters of the hotel pool. I spun in that direction only to find it didn't open until nine, so I just kept running.

At least the dark-gray cloud cover provided some relief from the heat.

I should have checked with the front desk for a good route. Instead, I followed my nose. I loved a good view while running, so I headed toward the beach. The boardwalk would be a fun run anyway, so I aimed for that.

As I approached the park, which led to the beach, I noticed another runner coming from the opposite direction. She wasn't too hard to notice, with a bright-pink top and leggings. While shorter than me, she was making good time and moving quickly. Then I recognized her—Erica Wheeler, the mayor's wife. I waved and called out, "Hey, Erica!"

We met up on the sidewalk across from the park, jogging in place as we waited for the light to turn. "Good morning, Jackie. I'm guessing you, like me, needed to burn off some of this stress and anxiety."

I was impressed. She'd managed that entire phrase without huffing or puffing like I was. "Definitely. Plus, I've added running as a good habit"—*pant, pant*—"to replace a bad one."

She glanced over. "Oh. That's a good idea." She checked her watch. "How far into the run are you?"

"Just started. You?"

"Same." Once it was safe, she glanced both ways, and we ran across the street.

"I wasn't certain of the best route," I said, struggling to keep up with her pace. "Do you have a usual route?"

"I do. Usually down to the end of the boardwalk—where the event tent is set up—then up and down the nearby pier, down the length of the boardwalk, and across this park and back home. Most of it's a beautiful view." Since we'd reached the beach, she waved her arm at the gulf.

I smiled, enjoying the feel of the breeze on my face, the sound of the waves, and the seagulls. This was a peaceful place, even if someone had died there just the night before. We passed the event staging, the food and game booths, and headed down the pier. I was concerned about running with water on both sides but figured the wooden handrail should protect against clumsiness.

It was interesting to run on the pier. The wood gave more than cement, making my stride feel bouncier and less jarring. I listened to the thumping, rhythmic sound of our steps, which we managed to do in unison.

"I should run with a partner more often," I managed to gasp out when we reached the end and turned back around. "It definitely increases my pace."

Erica nodded, sweat dripping off her face. "It does. Would your brother go with you?"

I laughed, although it came out more like a cough. "Daniel doesn't believe in exercise for exercise's sake. He does enjoy team sports, like Ultimate Frisbee and touch football. How about Mayor Tom?"

She rolled her eyes. "He would never sweat in public. God forbid a constituent see him not at his best. No, he pays a physical trainer to keep him in shape."

There was some heat behind her words. I opted not to reply, plus it was *really* hard to keep up a conversation. After leaving the pier, we ran in silence down a long stretch of boardwalk that led toward the shops and restaurants.

To the left was the beach and the gulf, which occasionally cut in under the boardwalk with small, shallow inlets. To the right was a large dirt parking lot, bordered by fluorescent orange temporary fencing. I frowned as I noticed that the long length of fencing was uninterrupted.

"Why aren't there breaks in the fencing? How does someone get to the boardwalk from the parking lot?" I asked.

Erica puffed out a breath. "Tom had that put up last week to funnel people directly to the festival area. There have already been tons of complaints from the tourists and the shop owners."

"No wonder," I said as we approached the shops and restaurants. It would be incredibly annoying to have to walk all the way back just to get on the boardwalk and head back up toward the shops.

"He says the festival needs to make money so we can pave the parking area to bring in more tourists, more business."

The boardwalk made a sharp right to match the curve of the water as we reached the more populated area. At least, it would be populated later today. Currently, rows of empty benches lined the boardwalk on the beach side, patiently waiting for visitors to claim their spots and enjoy the view. To the right were the restaurants and stores, also patiently waiting for customers. I made a note to check out some of the tourist shops later to buy something for April.

Luckily, I didn't see any orange fencing in the breaks between buildings, so access to the lot would be easier. Evidently, the mayor had only paid for one side of the parking area to be fenced in.

When we left the boardwalk and entered the park, my knees complained about the switch from wood to cement. My entire body cheered when Erica's phone chimed, and she stopped to check the message.

Standing on one leg, she managed to balance for quad stretches, holding her foot behind her back in one hand and the phone in her other. I held on to a nearby rusted lamp post and followed her lead on the stretching.

"I wonder what's wrong," she said, concern in her eyes as she lifted them from the screen.

"Your husband?" I asked.

"Yes. He said there's an emergency and asked if I could come to the office."

"I hope it's not about Heather," I said, my gut clenching. Maybe they'd found out it *had* been poison.

"Oh. I'm not sure I'm ready to learn the answer." She bit her lower lip. "Can you come with me, just in case? Town Hall is on the route anyway."

"Sure. I'm still ready to help Redding Beach."

Like most of the buildings in the area, Town Hall had seen better days. Made of bricks that had once been painted white, the building was squat, square, and sad. Now the white paint was stained and chipped.

Not everything was old though. On the wall just beside the front door, a shiny keypad lock gleamed. Since Erica was shorter than me by a good six inches, I was able to see her input the code. While I tried not to pay attention, it was hard not to notice the pattern. And even harder not to react when I saw it was 1-2-3-4.

Erica glanced over her shoulder when she heard me snort. "I know, right? Tom doesn't like carrying keys, and he never bothered to change the default code for the entrance or the alarm. Luckily, Redding Beach isn't full of burglars desperate to break in." We stepped into a nondescript foyer. A picture of Mayor Tom hung on the wall in front of us and hallways led to the right and the left.

"Can we stop by the restroom before we go to his office?" I asked, wanting to wash off some of this sweat. Unlike Mayor Tom, I didn't mind people seeing me not at my best, but I did have some standards.

Erica had been heading down the hall to the right but switched directions and went to the left. "Of course."

I grabbed a bunch of paper towels from the dispenser, wet them, and gratefully wiped away the perspiration. I took off my cap, smoothed down my hair, and decided that was good enough. Erica did a similar routine.

"Okay, let's go find out the emergency," Erica said.

Fortunately, there were no police officers waiting for us in Mayor Tom's office. Just one frazzled mayor.

He immediately ran to his wife, clutched her arm. "Oh, thank God you're here, Erica. Alison Gerth just cancelled on me. What are we going to do?"

"Oh no!" Erica said.

"Who is Alison Gerth?" I asked, wondering if she had anything to do with the cooking contests.

Erica turned to me. "The town veterinarian. She and I were going to be the judges for the animal costume parade at eleven o'clock before the crab cake contest."

"It's terrible," Mayor Tom said. "Just one problem after another."

"I don't know who we could get to judge at this late notice," Erica said, flicking her eyes at the clock hanging nearby. "That's only three hours from now."

"I could do it," I offered. Erica and Tom turned to face me, hope blossoming in Erica's eyes.

"Are you sure?" she asked. "That would help us out. You could judge the animals first and then some food. What do you say?"

I smiled. "As long as I don't have to taste them. That would spoil my appetite for the crab cakes."

She smiled. "No chance of that." She turned to face her husband. "There, honey. Is that an okay solution?"

Like a light switch flipped, Mayor Tom's face went from panicked to pleased. "Thank you, Jackie, that's very kind of you." Then he tossed in a dash of charm. "And I'm sorry for my previous stressed state. Alison isn't the only one cancelling today. Several food vendors and crab cake contestants have cancelled as well. At least the ride and game operators are still coming." He sighed and walked behind his desk, dropping into a black leather chair. "I'm not certain why everyone is so worried. I'm sure what happened to Heather was an accident. Some unknown allergy or something." He frowned at the sleek phone on his desk. "But I can't find another judge for the food competition. I'm so pleased you both have agreed to stay on."

Erica and I exchanged glances. He hadn't actually asked me whether I wanted to or not. I suspected he hadn't given his wife the option either.

I checked the clock. "On that note, I should get back to the hotel and get ready."

At least this would be one contest where I didn't worry about being killed.

―――――

I was wrong. Everyone was trying to kill me. Kill me with cuteness that is.

The animals were just adorable and the costumes…so much fun. Big dogs, little dogs, grumpy cats, and grumpier cats, all dressed to look like crabs. There was even a ferret wearing a bib and fake hands holding a crab mallet and a claw cracker.

"How are we supposed to choose?" I asked Erica.

She smiled. "Well, *you* can go with the cutest animal, I guess. But even that is a difficult task."

"The corgi probably wins my vote," I admitted. "His owners sized the costume perfectly so his short little legs put the crab legs on the ground. But the beautiful gray tabby is tempting too." I struggled with my choice, then paused. "Wait. You said that's how *I* can choose. How are you choosing?"

Erica sighed. "I'm choosing based on who contributed more to my husband's mayoral campaign."

I frowned. Like the food tastings, they should have done something to guarantee impartial judging to prevent unfair influence. I said the same to her.

"I tried to tell him that," she said with an eye roll. "Anyway, you choose your favorite based on cuteness, and I'll worry about politics."

In the end, I ended up choosing the tabby. Both pets were cute, but the corgi looked like he was soaking up the attention and didn't mind the costume. The tabby, on the other hand, was…crabby. I figured if she had to suffer being in a costume, she should be rewarded. And because her owner—or should I say servant—was the wife of the head of the local VFW, Erica chose her as well.

"Connections and cuteness," I whispered to Erica as the mayor awarded the prize, a gift card to a local pet store, to the cat. "Uh-oh, looks like the corgi is demanding a recount."

The corgi had taken off, still wearing his costume, and streaked through the crowd, his leash dragging behind him. Pretty fast for such little legs. As he was heading toward me, I crouched and prepared to grab him or the leash.

A quick dodge to the left, and he raced past me and toward the cooking area. I noticed Benjy up ahead, talking to another contestant. "Grab that dog," I shouted.

"Looks more like a crab," he yelled back, grinning, but obediently bent down. The wily dog outsmarted him, ducking under the food truck and heading toward the long expanse of the boardwalk.

"Oh, I hope he doesn't go in the water," I panted.

Fortunately, he didn't seem interested in the beach and just kept running. We followed behind, barely gaining on him. Luckily the orange fencing kept him penned in on the right side.

The corgi-crab raced along in a straight line, easily passing surprised beachgoers. I had a harder time, occasionally ramming into someone with a quick apology. As we reached the right-hand turn, I glanced behind. The mayor and the corgi's owner were far behind us. Actually, there wasn't an us. I realized Benjy had disappeared.

I turned my focus back to the chase and skidded around the corner, desperate to catch up with the pup. Suddenly, about twenty feet in front of our escapee, Benjy ran out between two buildings, blocked the dog's path, and grabbed his leash. The dog wiggled for a few moments, then sat, grinning and panting. Obviously unrepentant.

"Where'd you come from?" I asked Benjy.

"I leaped over the fence and cut diagonally across the parking lot," he said as we headed back to the dog's owner. "It was clear we weren't going to get him if we kept going in a straight line."

"You jumped the fence?" I was impressed, then remembered. "Oh right. You did hurdles in high school, didn't you?"

He flushed. "In high school, yes. I was reminded today that I'm no longer in high school." As we retraced our path, he pointed to a section of fence that had seen better days. Not only had the post been ripped from the ground, but the orange fencing lattice was also ripped. "Oops. I landed badly but was able to scramble up quickly."

I noticed he was limping slightly. "You still saved the dog. And this is just temporary fencing anyway." I picked up the fence post and shoved it back into the hole. It was loose but should work. The broken net at the top was a bigger issue. Luckily, Mayor Tom had waited for us after we came around the corner walking the dog, so he didn't see the torn netting.

"Thank you so much!" The owner hugged Benji. "Thank you for saving my naughty boy. Now, Peeper, you know better than to run off. That's rude," she said to the dog as she walked off.

The mayor looked hesitant but finally blurted out, "Thank you, Benjy," before darting off.

"That looked like it hurt to say," Benji commented. "I think he suspects I did something to the soup. He wasn't happy when he announced I would be first for the tasting today. I'm glad I had finished everything before having to chase a wayward crabdog."

"Again? How did that happen?"

"Same way as last time. The mayor put everyone's names in a bowl. He wasn't happy when he drew my name first. Especially since he's now the third judge. Apparently, he couldn't find anyone else."

On one hand, I was impressed with the mayor's bravery, or more probable, his desperation. On the other hand, if he was the killer, he didn't have anything to worry about.

Benjy shook his head. "I still have no idea what happened to

Heather. I didn't put any ingredients in that soup that would have made her sick, much less kill her. And I didn't notice anyone lurking around the soup either."

"Is that what you told the police?"

"Yes. It's the truth. I don't lie."

That last statement was obviously for my benefit.

"Okay, okay. I made a mistake back then. I have no idea why I trusted Heather over you. One of the stupidest things I did in my life, and I didn't have alcohol to blame. But, Benjy, I think you have bigger problems to worry about right now."

"You mean the fact that my cooking killed someone? Or the fact the media is basically telling the world that my previous restaurant closed due to E.coli?"

"At least no one died that time."

"Thanks, Jackie. A chef loves to hear that about his food. 'At least no one died.'" He sighed, looking out at the water. "I wasn't even working there at the time, actually. That was while Kimi was really ill, and I had taken a long-term sabbatical to be with her and my sister. You'll notice the reporters didn't mention that fact."

I placed my hand on his arm. "No, they left that part out. And unfortunately, the public doesn't bother to do their own research. I had that happen to me. I was arrested one evening for being drunk and disorderly, and the media played it out like I was on drugs. I wasn't quite that stupid. But sales at my restaurant started declining the next evening. And never recovered."

Benjy whipped his phone out of his pocket and brandished it. "My sous chef already texted me that over half of our reservations cancelled for tonight. And all of our Sunday brunch reservations cancelled."

"Oof. I know that hurts." Especially because he had probably already set the staff schedule, so he'd pay more in salaries than he would earn, and he'd have to make up the difference in lost tips to his servers. "Well, if there was poison in the soup, hopefully, the police will find out who put it there, and you'll be exonerated." I suddenly became aware that I was gently rubbing his arm. I let go and backed up.

"I hope so. Officer Mallory didn't inspire confidence."

"Neither did Officer Short."

Benjy snorted. "You and your nicknames for people."

"No, that's really his name. I almost laughed when he said it since, yeah, I was already calling him that." Benjy was familiar with this habit of mine. I had nicknamed all of the faculty based on some unique characteristic of their personality or looks. There was Chef Dirty Apron, Chef Grumpy, and Chef Toupee.

As we approached the tent, I frowned. There weren't many people around when there should have been hundreds, although I did spot my brother and Skylar, who was wearing all black today. While there were still a few minutes for the audience to arrive, that wasn't the main problem. "The mayor said some competitors dropped out, but I didn't realize this many. What, we're down to seven from the original fifteen?"

Benjy sighed. "I'm guessing they didn't want their restaurants to be affiliated with a deadly festival." He sighed. "I don't have that luxury becasue I'm already connected. Sofia Delgado is staying, perhaps due to loyalty to me since she used to work for me. I tried Sofia's crab cake, and it's incredible. Sure to be the winner. I didn't think she could improve on the one she created as my sous chef, but she did. Here, come meet her." He dragged me over to a petite woman in chef's whites who was putting the finishing touches on her crab cake display. Her lustrous brown hair was pulled back into a ponytail. She glanced briefly in our direction before swiftly returning her focus to her plating.

"Sofia, I wanted to make certain you had a chance to talk to our illustrious judge. Jackie, this is the awesome Sofia Delgado."

Even if I didn't allow Benjy's opinion to influence me, my eyes convinced me Sofia should win. "Your crab cake looks amazing," I stepped around it, looking at it from all angles. She had taken mini crabcakes and wrapped them with incredibly thin ribbons of avocado. The juxtaposition of the bright green avocado with the perfectly browned crab cake was striking. It smelled delicious too.

And she was as gorgeous as her crab cake. I felt a stab of jealousy when Benjy pulled her into a one-armed hug but realized I was being irrational. Benjy wasn't mine to be jealous of. And I knew him. There was no way he would have dated her when she had been his sous chef. Although...what about now? I swallowed any unkind thoughts and smiled at her. "I can't wait to taste this."

Sofia flushed, I assumed in pleasure or embarrassment or both. She shyly raised her eyes from her prep table. "Thank you, Chef Jackie. That means a lot, coming from you."

"You're welcome," I said, then noticed the mayor was waving me over. "I think it's time to start the tasting. Good luck to both of you."

"Yeah, I could use some," Benjy said, heading toward his prep area.

I could use some as well, I thought. I'd be the one eating the food and risking my life.

I walked over to Daniel on the way to the judges' table. I had texted him about the animal contest, but because he was sadly allergic to anything fuzzy or furry, he'd declined to join.

He wore his usual dark jeans with a blue polo shirt, but the dark circles under his eyes concerned me. "Didn't you get any sleep?"

He shrugged.

"Worried about me?"

"For many reasons. Aren't you nervous about judging this food today?"

"I am *now*. I suppose I would feel a lot better if we had an answer from the police. Was she poisoned? Was she not?"

"Perhaps you should step down as a judge. Stay safe."

"Safe, but without any prospects. This festival, small as it is, could give me some exposure and publicity I need to get back on the map. Plus...I promised the mayor I would judge, Daniel. I need to keep my promises."

He didn't look surprised, just gave me a quick hug and wished me luck.

I hoped I wouldn't need it.

chapter eight

. . .

WHEN I SAT at the tasting table, I was dismayed to see more TV news camera crews on hand than audience members. The news stations, I realized, were here to film the tasting, just in case there was another death. Nothing better for ratings than murder and mayhem.

Greg, from the Gourmet Channel, caught my eye and raised an eyebrow. I smiled back, grateful to have at least one cameraperson who wasn't just here for the thrill factor.

Erica sat in her chair, smoothing down her dress. She was, once again, in neutral colors, this time a pale-gray dress with matching heels and a sparkling beaded necklace. She took the leftmost seat, giving Tom the middle chair. She was probably used to giving him center stage.

I took a deep breath, trying to relax and appreciate the amazing aromas of good food: the sweet smell of crab, of course, but also red peppers, the zesty scent of citrus, and the heavy aroma of frying oils. I was happy not to smell any almond this time.

"Thank you to everyone who came out today, especially considering the tragedy that happened yesterday," Mayor Tom began as he stood at the podium. "Before we start, I'd like to have a thirty-second pause in remembrance of Heather Curtis."

That seemed like such a thoughtful thing to do. I wondered if it was his idea or his wife's. I bowed my head and tried to come up with happy memories of the deceased. By the time the thirty seconds were up, I'd only managed to recall one time, an instance when she'd lent me her sharpening steel.

"I thank everyone for that tribute." Tom straightened his tie. "Although we are still without answers, I'm certain we'll learn that Heather had an unknown allergy to something in the crab soup."

I glanced at Daniel. He mouthed, "Cyanide." I frowned at him and turned my attention back to the mayor.

"And having met Heather and spent time with her, I know the best way to honor her memory is to continue this festival that meant so much to her."

"So much to you," Erica muttered under her breath.

"Fortunately, our two other lovely judges are here and ready to judge the crab cake competition. Even better, I get to enjoy all these tasty creations our fantastic competitors have cooked up for us."

Lovely, tasty, fantastic. Tom certainly knew his adjectives. I couldn't wait to hear him critique the food. That is, assuming the food didn't kill any of us.

"A reminder, we will judge the crab cakes based on taste, presentation, and creativity. First up is…"—he paused, adjusted his tie—"Chef Benjy Hayes. Chef, please describe your offering for this competition." He stepped away from the podium and settled into his seat.

Benjy cleared his throat. "Thank you, Mayor Tom. I present to you my crispy crab cake. Rather than using breadcrumbs for binding, I used kettle potato chips. Please enjoy." He set three plates on the table.

You'd think he had set down live hand grenades by how we reacted to those crab cakes. Stalling, I swiveled the plate to the right to see the crab cake from all angles. Since it was perfectly round and flat, that really did nothing but delay the moment one of us would put the food in our mouth and find out if we lived.

The mayor and his wife also hesitated to actually taste the crab cake. Erica was brave enough to pick up her fork but paused, glancing at the two of us.

"It's beautiful," I began, swiveling the plate to the left. "I can see a nice crust on the outside, which will provide a textural element." I used the side of my fork to cut a section of crab cake. Stared at it.

No one moved. Realizing how bad this looked for Benjy and hoping that despite breaking up with him, he didn't hold anything against me, I took a bite. I could feel everyone's eyes on me: the press, the mayor, Erica, Benjy, the other contestants. All waiting to see if I had a reaction. Despite the seriousness of the situation, some morbid side of my sense of humor thought I should grab at my throat. But the saner, kinder side reminded me that someone really had passed away, and this wasn't a time for practical joking.

Instead, I swallowed, slowly reached for my water glass, and took a drink. "Textbook perfect. I appreciate that you used very little filler, which lets the sweetness of the crab shine through."

I must have inspired Erica, who took a taste from the plate in front of her. "I agree with Jackie. The taste of the crab is foremost. That hard crust and the chips inside contrast nicely with the tender texture of the crab."

Having watched two women taste the crab and not die, Mayor Tom evidently felt brave enough to try a teeny, tiny piece of the crab cake. "It tastes good."

Benjy waited for a beat, as we all did, wondering if Tom would elaborate, but that appeared to be the extent of his opinion.

"Thank you very much, judges." He took the plates and went back to his station. I saw him take a deep breath.

"Next up is Chef Veronica Rossi, owner of the Pasta n' Boots restaurant chain." This time, Tom's voice was full of energy and enthusiasm.

"Thank you, Mayor Tom," said the pretty chef, the one I had noticed the first night with the striking, although obviously not natural, reddish-orange hair color. "I have prepared for you a red pepper and onion crab cake with a red pepper coulis."

I wondered if she had chosen the sauce to match her hair. The crab cake wasn't bad, but there were problems. Since it was my job, I shared them. "The crab cake is good, well-seasoned. The sauce is also good and complements the crab cake nicely."

Veronica beamed at me. I felt bad that I was about to remove that smile.

"However, by drowning the crab cake in the sauce, you ruined the crisp outside you got from the pan."

Erica nodded. "I agree. It's a shame since the crab cake is now soggy. The sauce is quite good. I enjoyed the tang. From sour cream, I believe?"

Veronica nodded and turned to Tom.

"It's very tasty."

Veronica pivoted, her ponytail bouncing as she returned to her spot.

The next few tastings went similarly. I'd give my opinion with critique and praise. "Nice pairing." "Needs salt." "The acidity of the sauce really boosted the flavor."

Erica would then agree, sometimes expanding on what I said, occasionally adding her own opinion. The further we went on, the bolder she became.

And Mayor Tom continued adding such culinary insights such as "delicious," "tasty," "I liked it," and one "yummy." Erica and I exchanged eye rolls at that last one. Although to give him credit, that was Sofia Delgado's beautiful avocado crab cake, and it was, in fact, quite yummy.

"Next up is James Sickels, from Redding Beach's own Jimbo's BBQ and Pies." When James set the plates in front of me, I winced. The crab cakes were served on buns that shined with grease and the crab cakes within looked sad and wilted. I lifted the top bun. The slathered-on mayonnaise wasn't going to help. Rather than eat it with the bun and gobs of mayo, I forked some up and tasted it. The crab cake tasted the way it looked: gray and greasy. And seemed to be mostly breadcrumbs, with some mayonnaise and a little crab holding it together. I swallowed, then waited for Erica or Tom to start this time.

"This brings me back. Just like Mama would make," Tom said.

"Me too," I said, not admitting that my mama was a terrible cook.

Erica bit her lip as she glanced at her husband. Then she took a deep breath and blurted out, "I think we would have been able to evaluate it better without the bun or extra mayonnaise. But I see why you sell plenty of these at your restaurant."

As we adjourned to the back of the tent to discuss the competition, I whispered to her, "Because no one in Redding Beach has good taste?"

She giggled but quickly fell silent after stealing a glance at her husband.

Mayor Tom went back to the podium. "Thank you so much, competitors, for your delicious contributions. Please excuse the judges for a few minutes as we adjourn to our judging area and determine who should win our first crab cake contest! Again, we are looking at taste, presentation, and creativity."

We "adjourned" to a place about twenty feet from the table, just past one of the outside tent poles. I turned to face my fellow judges so no one could read my lips.

"First place is a no-brainer," I whispered.

Erica nodded sagely.

"James Sickels," Mayor Tom said.

"What?" Erica and I asked simultaneously.

"It was good," Mayor Tom defended.

"Now, Tom, admit it. You're only voting for it because it was cooked by a local chef," Erica said. "It was greasy and mushy."

"Veronica's was mushy too."

"At least hers started out life crispy." Realizing I was raising my voice, I drew closer to Erica and Tom and spoke softly. "But then the sauce made it mushy. Sickel's was always a mess. He cooked it at too low a temperature. And it was fifty percent bread crumbs, forty percent mayonnaise, and maybe ten percent crab."

"So, which one do *you* think should win first place?" Mayor Tom asked, pouting.

"Sofia's," Erica and I said, again simultaneously.

"Really?" Mayor Tom asked, surprised. "I thought the best tasting was Ben—" He stopped, cleared his throat. "I mean, Sofia's."

"Benjy's was the best tasting," I agreed. "But Sofia Delgado's avocado crab cake was a close second in taste and was more creative with a gorgeous presentation. It therefore deserves first place."

"Although Benjy's technique was textbook perfect," Erica said. She played with her necklace. "Maybe we should award him first."

Mayor Tom shook his head. "No. After yesterday, I think it might be best if we don't draw attention to Mr. Hayes."

I saw red but suppressed my anger. "I would think, after yesterday, it would be good to send some good publicity Mr. Hayes's way."

"You would think that." Tom peered down his nose. "I believe I heard that you two used to date. Perhaps you need to recuse yourself from this decision."

I took a quick step back but refused to answer, knowing if I started, I might not stop.

Surprisingly, Erica spoke up. "I never dated him, Tom, and I also think that if we don't give Benjy first, he should be the second-place choice."

He sighed. "Fine. I hope we didn't just reward a murderer. Who gets third place?"

"Veronica Rossi," Erica said.

I concurred.

"Even though the crab cake was mushy?" Tom asked, confused.

"Yes," I said. "Texture is important, but taste rules all. The red pepper paired nicely with the crab."

He shrugged. "Fine, let me go announce the winners." He stood and moved to the microphone in the center of the stage.

I locked eyes with Benjy, who appeared worried. I decided to give him some advance notice. I casually brushed my fingers across my face, one above my lips and the other against my chin. He smiled, clearly getting my secret message.

It reminded me of when we were dating. I swear, it was like he could read my mind. Most of the time that had been useful, but I'd never been able to hide anything from him.

"Ladies and gentlemen, we have our winners," the mayor began. He paused to wait for the crowd, as little as it was, to quiet. He took three envelopes out of his pocket, which I knew contained financial prizes. Not much, but everything helped in the restaurant business. "In first place, we have Chef Sofia Delgado with her avocado crab cake."

The crowd cheered as the young woman ran up to collect her prize. I leaned over to Erica. "Why'd he do first place first? That's usually the finale."

She rolled her eyes. Having watched their marital relationship for a couple of days now, I suspected Erica was at high risk for a repetitive-motion eye injury.

"And in second place," the mayor began. "We have…Chef Veronica Rossi, with her red pepper sauce crab cake."

Oh no, he didn't.

chapter nine

. . .

HE DID. *He stole second place from Benjy.*

I closed my eyes and said a quick Serenity Prayer to calm myself down. Obviously, Mayor Tom was one of those things I'd need to accept I couldn't change.

"And in third place," Tom hurried to say, even while the crowd was still applauding, "is Benjy Hayes with his crispy crab cake."

Benjy looked more confused than angry when he accepted his third-place award. That was okay. I was annoyed enough to cover for him. Tom seemed to sense that, so he hurried over to talk to the press.

I turned to Erica instead. "Did that just happen?"

She rubbed at her temples. "It did. I'm sorry. Tom's probably going to claim he forgot. Or that he made an executive decision. Something like that." She turned to face me. "I apologize for my husband's behavior. I'll try to address it tonight, but I can't promise anything."

"It's not your fault," I muttered. "But thanks for the apology. And I suspect both you and I will be pulling for Benjy tomorrow."

She smiled, which transformed her features from plain to pretty. "I will be. And hopefully, they'll discover that whatever happened to Heather had nothing to do with Benjy. In fact, I see Detective Preston over there."

I followed her gaze and saw the homicide detective standing just inside the tent with Officer Short and Officer Tall.

He seemed to be waiting for Mayor Tom. Since that was the case, I walked over to Benjy. "I'm sorry."

Benjy had already opened the envelope and was tucking the money order into his wallet. "Don't be. Third place is fine. But did I misinterpret your signal?"

"You didn't. Mayor Tom changed what we'd agreed upon. You were supposed to get second and Veronica was third."

"I suspect that as long as we don't know what killed Heather, Tom isn't my biggest fan. I'm glad you liked my crab cake. As you know, I was expecting Sofia to win this round. She's amazing. She was my first hire at Kimi's Kitchen, and when she left to start her own place, I was happy for her but sad for me. Her restaurant is struggling, as many are, and a win might give her a boost. I doubt a win will do much for me, especially after Heather's death."

"I do hope you get rid of this cloud of suspicion over your head."

"The man that could bring about that weather change, Detective Preston, just pulled Mayor Tom to the side. They both seem serious."

I joined Benjy in watching the two men. The police detective said something to Tom that caused the mayor to jerk his head up and take a step back.

"Something shook him up," Benjy said. "I wonder what."

When Tom returned to the podium, I thought we might find out.

"Thanks to everyone for coming today to the crab cake competition. Please visit our vendors and our local shops and restaurants. Join us tomorrow evening at five p.m. for our crab freestyle competition, when the chefs let their creativity fly! Or since these are crabs, I guess I should say swim."

The crowd laughed weakly.

"Thank you very much. I do ask that everyone leave the tent as quickly as possible to allow us to set up for tomorrow."

Since nothing had to change for tomorrow, I suspected this was Tom's way of chasing away the press. Greg gave me a quick salute as he left the tent.

My pulse quickened as Detective Preston approached, but he

turned first to Benjy. "Mr. Hayes, can you follow me to the station, please? Ms. Norwood, if you can arrive in two hours, that would be appreciated."

It was a good sign, I hoped, that the detective allowed us to find our own way to the police station rather than taking us there in a police car. Presumably, that meant he'd let us leave as well.

I spent the next two hours alternating between worrying about Benjy and worrying about myself. While I knew that neither Benjy nor I had killed Heather, I wasn't certain Detective Preston knew that. And the fact we were being pulled in for questioning pointed toward there definitely having been something suspicious in Benjy's soup.

Had they even had enough time to do an autopsy on Heather? I shuddered, picturing her body on that sterile table. I'd watched enough CSI-type shows to imagine what they'd do to her. Those one-hour shows always exaggerated how quick the process was. Heather had only died yesterday, though it felt like so much longer.

I didn't have a car, so I used a rideshare service to get to the police station. The driver gave me some side-eye when I got in his car, probably wondering about my police station destination. In preparation for my interview, I'd worn my traditional hide-my-celebrity-status outfit of sunglasses and a baseball cap. I'd paired that with ripped jeans and a black sleeveless top.

When I stepped inside, I took off the cap, ran my fingers through my hair, and pulled my hair back into a ponytail. The officer at the desk told me to take a seat in the waiting room and that Detective Preston would be with me shortly.

The Redding Beach police station wasn't like those television shows with their slick modern sets. No, this looked more like an old office space, with water-stained ceiling tiles, chipped linoleum, and beat-up furniture. No wonder Mayor Tom was trying to inject some money into the town. I frowned. Maybe Daniel had a point. Why would Tom have committed murder if it would ruin his festival? But if not him, who would have been trying to kill Erica? I was convinced by now that Erica was the intended victim since no one could have predicted the cameraman would make everyone swap places.

Unless…it was the cameraman. Had Greg poisoned the bowl of soup? For what reason? Greg worked for Gourmet Channel, meaning he had probably interacted with Heather. Exposure to Heather made me want to kill her when I saw her regularly, so I wouldn't be surprised if a Gourmet Channel staff member was brought to murder by her actions.

When my name was called, I quickly dismissed those thoughts and cleared my throat. "Hello, Detective Preston." As he led me through the door, I glanced around for Benjy but didn't see him. I hope it didn't mean he was locked up somewhere.

Detective Preston opened the door and stepped aside to allow me to enter first. This room was even dingier than the waiting room. One narrow table, two ancient plastic chairs on opposite sides, and everything older than me. Then again, this was the interrogation room—I assumed—so they probably weren't concerned about aesthetics.

I sat and scooted the chair away from the table. That was for naught since Detective Preston then brought his chair even closer, removing any trace of personal space. He placed a thick file on the table and opened it.

"Before we get started, I'd like to Mirandize you." Preston pulled a card out of his wallet, then read the Miranda Warning from the card.

Between being terrified I was being arrested, I wondered why, after presumably being a cop for years, he had to read the card.

"Do you understand the rights I have just read to you? With these rights in mind, do you wish to speak to me?" Preston finished.

"Do I actually have a choice?" I asked, then immediately regretted it.

"Yes," Preston said without breaking eye contact.

"I do understand, and yes, I do wish to speak to you so we can find out what happened." There. That sounded good. I hoped.

"Thank you. Could you state your full name for the record?"

"Jacqueline Isabelle Norwood." I missed being able to add of *Dinner, Drinks, and Decadence*.

"Can you please go over the events of yesterday, Friday, May thirteenth?"

For what felt like the fiftieth time, I recited what had happened the day before, remembering this time to mention Greg's switcheroo with the seating.

"You mentioned that you and your brother went to the competitor's area. Did you or your brother"—he checked his notepad—"Daniel Norwood, ever touch anything?"

"We did not," I said firmly.

"I have a witness who stated that you lifted the lid of one of the crockpots. Do you deny that?"

Well, shoot. I did do that. "I totally forgot about that until now. I detected Indian spices coming from one of the pots, and I tracked it down. I just lifted the lid, smelled it, then put the lid back on. I do that sort of thing all the time."

He checked his notes again. "The witness stated that you opened the lid, moved your hand above the soup, then put the lid back on."

"I was wafting the odor in my direction. You learn pretty quickly not to place your nose over a hot liquid unless you want to ruin your hard work with nasal drip. That also wasn't Benjy's soup."

"The witness was unable to confirm or deny that."

"Great, your witness notices details such as hand waving but not where I was standing." I shifted in the uncomfortable seat. "Besides, how would that have resulted in poisoning Heather's bowl? Assuming there was a poison," I added.

Detective Preston pulled a paper out of the folder. "The lab confirmed there was cyanide in the soup."

I guess Daniel should feel validated his research was right. But how did the cyanide get in Heather's bowl?

"It wasn't just in Heather's bowl," the detective said after a dramatic pause. "It was in the entire pot."

chapter ten
...

IT TOOK a moment to process his words. "You mean, I could have been killed as well?"

He raised an eyebrow. "You could have, had you immediately tasted the soup rather than sniffed it."

Realizing he was implying that the delay in tasting the food was to avoid the poison, I stopped thinking about my barely avoided death and defended myself. "I always 'sniff' food before eating. First of all, delaying the initial taste increases salivation and anticipation. Second of all, it's a game of sorts for me to try and identify ingredients by smell alone. And third, much of what we experience as taste actually comes from scent."

"Still," he slowly drawled, "it sure was convenient."

"You're right. If I hadn't delayed tasting, death would have been very inconvenient."

The detective was good at the impassive face thing, but he might have had a hint of amusement at my response.

I continued. "Honestly, Detective, any chef worth their salt should have done the same. I'm surprised Heather didn't." I considered for a minute. "Knowing her, it was so she could be the first to critique the soup."

"Which she did, right?"

"Yes. She said it was silky. To die for." I swallowed to clear the lump in my throat. "Then she did."

In the ensuing silence, I remembered something. "Wait, let me show you." I pulled out my cell phone, went to YouTube, and pulled up old videos of my show. I fast-forwarded until I found what I wanted. "Look."

Pushing play, I showed the end, "the bite," as they called it, where I tasted the food I had prepared. That episode, I had prepared salmon in a yogurt sauce. Past Me picked up a forkful, lifted it to my nose while inhaling deeply, and only then took a bite. I showed him two more videos where I did the same thing.

Now I took a deep breath—to steady myself rather than draw in the scent of food—and turned back to Detective Preston. "So unless you think that I have spent the last few years creating this habit in preparation to provide an alibi, I promise you I've always done this."

He tapped the table for a while, staring down at the phone. He inclined his head, seemingly accepting what I had said. "Would you say you and the deceased had an amicable relationship?" Preston asked, pen at the ready.

I snorted. Probably not the best reaction. "You've already asked this question in various ways. And no. That doesn't mean I wanted to kill her."

"How about the evening that she died? You mentioned the altercation in front of the mayor when you discovered she was also a judge. Was that the only issue between you and Ms. Curtis?"

Our conversation when she first spotted me in the tent hadn't been pleasant, but I saw no reason to share that with Detective Preston.

He checked his notes. "A witness has stated that earlier, before the tasting, you and the victim had been conversing. Apparently, the body language between the two of you indicated hostility and aggression."

I tensed, then, realizing my reactions were being scrutinized, deliberately relaxed. "A witness is analyzing body language now, are they?"

"They said they noticed you quickly and deliberately entering Ms. Curtis's personal space."

That cleared it up for me. Obviously, that was when Heather had taunted me about whether I could keep a husband or not. "Yes, Ms. Curtis had brought up my estranged husband."

Another check of his notes. "That would be Simon Levenson?"

"Yes. We're currently separated, which Ms. Curtis was aware of and was using to antagonize me."

Preston leaned in. I wanted to tell him he was entering my personal space, which indicated hostility and aggression. "Yet you say you had no motive to kill her?"

I did my best to not flinch back from his proximity and maintained steady eye contact with him. "No."

"You can't think of any?" He leaned back in his chair. I was happy to have my personal bubble back. "Wow, you must be more open-minded than I am."

This guy was annoying me, probably deliberately. "What's that supposed to mean?"

"Do you know who we found in her hotel room when we went there?"

I shrugged. "I have no idea who she's currently sleeping with. Can't say I care. When we were in culinary school, I stopped bothering to learn their names. She switched men too quickly."

Detective Preston just stared. He rose slowly, unfolding his lean body, and strode out of the room. A quick jerk of his head indicated I should follow him.

Curious, I did so. As we turned the corner to the waiting room, he came into view. Brown hair, red-rimmed brown eyes, shocked expression.

"Simon?" I asked, flabbergasted to see my soon-to-be-ex-husband. "Wait!" I turned back to Detective Preston. "It was *Simon* in her room?"

chapter eleven
. . .

I STALKED TOWARD SIMON. "You accused me of ruining our marriage and you were sleeping with Heather. How long?"

Simon winced. "It doesn't matter."

"It does matter."

He refused to answer, so I turned back to Detective Preston. "How long?"

Detective Preston pulled out his notebook. "He stated that he and the victim had been in a relationship for approximately three years."

Simon should be thankful we were in a police station, where I was already under suspicion for murder. If not, I might have killed him then and there. "That was right after we got married! Before I even started drinking heavily. You blamed me for our marriage ending, and you've been cheating on me for most of it!" I could hear my heart pounding in my ears.

"She came onto me."

"No kidding! She was always competing with me for everything. And what, you're completely innocent? You just laid there and thought of England?" What was it that Benjy had said? That Heather had wanted him because he was mine. Obviously, she'd done the same with Simon but had succeeded there.

I turned to Detective Preston. "You asked me if I was sorry Heather is dead. At that time, I said no. But you know what, I am sorry she's dead. If she was alive now, I could kill her." I swiveled on my heel and stormed out of the police station.

No one stopped me, so I figured I was done with Detective Preston. At least for now. I regretted my outburst the farther I got from the police station. I just threatened to kill a dead woman. *Great going, Jackie. That didn't make you look suspicious at all.*

Hopefully, the detective would realize my shocked reaction to finding out about Simon and Heather was sincere, which would actually lower my motive.

I *had* been shocked. I hadn't faked that at all. Here I was, worried I wasn't keeping my promises, and he couldn't even stick to that "remain faithful" promise.

As I stomped back to the hotel, I reflected on our relationship. Had there been any clues to his infidelity? I reduced my pace and wandered toward the water. Finding a bench, I sat and tried to slow my breathing and thinking. I couldn't remember any signs of his unfaithfulness. It was hard to notice anything under a blanket of drunkenness. I could barely recall what *I* had done in the months leading up to rehab. How could I remember what Simon had done?

He'd had plenty of opportunity while I'd been traveling around the country promoting my various *Dinner, Drinks, and Decadence* cookbooks. When I'd been home, things were bad between us. He'd been nasty and berated me constantly. I had accepted the abuse, figuring I deserved it.

Turns out, he'd been cheating on me all along. My behavior probably helped him assuage his guilt. That is, assuming he felt any.

Whereas I had felt like a total failure. Losing the show and my restaurant had been devastating. But the worst day was when I had received the divorce papers. No one got divorced in my family. Even my parents, who had a hideous marriage and drank more than I ever had, were still married.

I suppose I should, oddly enough, find comfort in the fact that it wasn't just me who caused the end of my marriage. I was so angry at Simon. Not just for the cheating, which was bad enough, but for gaslighting me, telling me the marriage was ending due to my behavior and my drinking. Getting that divorce notice on my birthday and during rehab was horrible. I had thought I had already hit rock bottom and was climbing back up, and then Simon knocked me back down again. It had taken even more effort to try and claw my way back.

And now, once again, my life was headed toward the toilet, thanks to a possible murder charge. I slumped down farther on the bench.

"Are you okay?" a young voice asked. "Your body language indicates you're unhappy."

Glancing up, I spotted Skylar. With her red hair in two braids, she looked younger than she had yesterday. I sighed as realization struck me. "You're the body-language witness."

"I apologize if my talking to the police detective made things uncomfortable for you. But I've been taught to cooperate with the police, that it's our moral obligation. I just told them what I noticed between you and Heather."

"I get that," I said, unable to be angry at the girl or her honesty.

"I still can't believe she's dead."

"Neither can I. But I didn't do it." I patted the bench next to me.

She sighed in relief as she sat down. "I'm very glad to hear that. You and Heather were my favorite chefs. I didn't like seeing the two of you fight, and it was worse when I thought you might have killed her. And your body language when I came up to get Heather's autograph indicated you were very angry. I hadn't said anything, so I know the anger wasn't directed at me."

"Are you some type of body-language expert or something?"

Skylar barked a laugh. "No. Somewhat the opposite. I'm bad with body language. I have autism. And when I was a child—"

"You're still a child. What are you, sixteen?"

"Seventeen as of last month. But when I was younger, I had limited social skills, didn't pick up social cues, or really understood or experienced emotions. I still struggle with this, but I've been working with a behavioral therapist, and she's taught me how to look for and interpret body language so I can recognize when someone is frustrated or bored with the topic I'm discussing. I tend to fixate on things."

"So now you're super observant about people's body language?" That skill went with her Super Fan nickname, which I now felt guilty for calling her.

"I'm more aware of when people are getting irritated. When I can tell people are getting bored or upset when I'm talking, I go away. Are you upset with me for talking to the police?"

"No." Well, maybe.

"You said that automatically, but your forehead is still wrinkled. That's an indicator of irritation," Skylar pointed out.

Trying to relax and empty my face of emotional cues, I focused on the soothing sounds of waves, gentle breezes, and seagulls before addressing her again. "I'm irritated at the situation. But since I didn't kill her, and I want other people to know I didn't kill her, I'm all for getting to the truth. Maybe something you told the police will help figure out the real killer."

"Perhaps. Although I've been reading statistics about the homicide clearance rate—meaning how many homicides are solved." She paused and carefully scanned my face.

"Go on."

"I'm sorry. I'm over-explaining things again, aren't I? Sorry."

I had to admire her self-awareness. I was almost twice her age, and I hadn't achieved that yet. "It's fine. Continue."

"Anyway, the national average is about sixty-one percent solved. However, Texas appears to be beating that average, at least as of five years ago, which was the most recent data I was able to find. They managed sixty-six point seven percent. Interestingly enough, the vast majority of the murders were with firearms."

"I can believe that."

"Of course, you can. Statistics don't lie. So firearms account for seventy-five percent of murders. Then another eleven percent were with knives or other cutting objects. Hands, feet, and fists account for another five percent, and blunt objects are around two percent. The remaining percentage, six point six percent, the murder weapon was listed as unknown or other. Others include fire, drugs, strangulation… and poison." She opened her eyes wide, staring into space. "So Heather's murder will probably be classified as other."

"You assume it was poison?" I asked, wondering what she knew.

"I believe so. I researched various poisons."

"Of course you did," I said, smiling to remove the sting.

"I told you I fixate on stuff." She bounced a knee. "Anyway, I knew Heather didn't have allergies, so I put all her symptoms into a search. It sounded like poison to me, cyanide specifically. I wasn't close enough to smell bitter almonds, did you?"

"I did."

"Not everyone can. Evidently, the ability to detect that odor is a recessive gene, so approximately one in four people can't smell it. I've never had the opportunity to test myself."

"I hope you never do, Skylar. I wish I hadn't smelled it either."

"Oh. Yes, I suppose you would feel that way." She peered at me intently. "Are you scared?"

"Of what? Being the next victim? Or going to jail for a murder I didn't commit? Yes to both." It was refreshing to talk to Skylar. Unlike most people I knew, she was straightforward and honest. It was easy to reciprocate.

"It must be difficult for you. I wish I could help."

I sat up straight and swiveled to face her, tucking a knee under a thigh. "Maybe you can. You watch people, right? And analyze their behavior so you can understand them better?"

"Well, not so much understand them because I don't experience emotions the same way as someone who is neurotypical. But yes."

"Have you noticed any other emotions from people connected to this case?"

"I know you and Erica were angry today at the tasting when Mayor Tom announced second place."

"How could you tell?"

"Your eyes widened, you sucked in a deep breath, and then you gave this fake-looking smile. Erica lifted her chin and glared at him. Those are all classic signs of anger."

"You *are* a body-language expert. And we *were* angry. We'd chosen Benjy for second place."

"Did Mayor Tom get confused?"

I wish I could be as optimistic as Skylar seemed about people's intentions. "No, he did it deliberately. He was worried we shouldn't be talking about Benjy right now because it was his soup that had the poison."

Staring at the nearby water, Skylar spoke slowly and carefully. "I don't think Benjy's the killer."

"I don't either. Why don't you? Is this still body language?"

She shook her head rapidly. "Not just that, although he always appears peaceful. His body is relaxed, as is his face. I like looking at him. And when I talked to him on Friday during the VIP event, he was very patient with me. I didn't see any signs of frustration or annoyance, even though we talked for a long time."

"What about?"

"Food."

"The science of food?"

She stopped bouncing her knee. "How did you know that?"

"Benjy studied it intensely during culinary school. He could talk about it for hours."

"Yes!" She beamed. "He knew more than I did." The smile dropped. "Sorry, my mother would have chastised me for sounding arrogant. It's just I've read lots and lots about the study of food. I took some online classes too."

"Are you planning on going to culinary school?" I thought she'd be great at it, with her knowledge and obvious love of food.

She shook her head slowly. "No, my parents don't think I should work in a kitchen, what with being on the spectrum."

"What do they want you to do? Stay home?"

"Maybe. My family has enough money that I don't need to work. Or I could be a vascular surgeon like my father."

"Well, I disagree with them, but never mind that. We need to find the killer." I mentally sorted through my possibilities. "So you saw that we were angry. How about right before Heather was killed? Did you notice anyone acting…say…nervous? Or anxious?" I figured anyone who knew they were about to kill someone—actually three someones if Erica and I had tried the soup—would exhibit signs.

She was quiet for a moment, probably rewinding things in her mind. I heard a speedboat buzzing out in the gulf, one very unhappy-sounding toddler, and a passing bus before she spoke up again. "Mayor Tom had jerky movements and spoke quickly. And most of the chefs were fidgety and had increased sweat, especially Chefs Veronica and Sofia. Although it was hot and muggy yesterday. Even I was sweating. That was just a physical response, though, not an emotional one."

"Anyone else?"

"Greg Wright also seemed on edge, but he always does. I've never seen him stand still. Maybe that's part of being a cameraman." She shrugged. "And when he made Heather and Erica swap seats, Heather had a pinched expression that normally means someone is trying to hide annoyance. Erica didn't seem bothered, but she was looking at the ground or the chairs as the seats were swapped, so I didn't really see."

I wanted to ask about the seat swap but remembered that was a moot point now. The entire pot was poisoned. It didn't matter about the bowls. Still… "Did you think it was odd that Greg made people switch seats?"

She shook her head, sending the braids flying. "No. I've seen him do things like that before at other events."

"Do you go to many of these?"

"Yes. As I said, my family has money. They're fine with me attending these food festivals and celebrity chef appearances, although usually someone travels with me. They don't usually attend themselves, preferring to stay at our home in Palo Alto. My tutor came with me this time but stayed in the hotel last night since the VIP event was extra."

"What did your mom and dad say about the murder?" They sounded like helicopter parents, so I'm sure a death would freak them out.

Skylar leaned forward, letting her hair obscure her face. "I didn't tell them."

I could barely hear her over the traffic. "You don't want them to know?"

"No, they'd probably want me to come home."

"Your tutor didn't tell them?"

"She didn't. If I had to guess, it's because she'd have to admit to not attending with me last night. I don't want them to know. I want to attend the festival. I was really relieved that it didn't get cancelled."

So Mayor Tom wasn't the only one who wanted the festival to continue. Admittedly, I did as well since that was the only way I'd get my full payment.

"I can't blame you for that," I admitted. "I didn't tell my parents either." I didn't bother telling her that I never talked to them anymore.

"Oh!" Skylar pulled out her phone. "My parents are calling me."

"Speak of the devil," I said.

"No, it's my parents," she said, hitting the talk button. "Hi, Dad. Yes, I'm safe. I'm just outside the hotel. Oh, you heard about that. Yeah, I guess I should have told you. Nothing happened today though. Yes, sir." She tucked the phone in her pocket. "I need to go back to the hotel room and call him again. Hopefully, he won't make us leave."

We both stood. "I hope not. There's only one day of the festival tomorrow, and *you* aren't the one eating the contestants' food. You should be fine."

She smiled. "I'll pass that on. Hope to see you tomorrow."

"I hope so too." With any luck, I wouldn't be arrested before then.

chapter twelve

. . .

I FOLLOWED Skylar back to the hotel, although more slowly, texting my brother to meet me in my hotel room. He was already at the door when I arrived.

"I need a hug," I said as we walked into the room.

Daniel, bless him, was always good for hugs. Broad shoulders and a firm but comforting grip.

"The police interview went badly?" he guessed as he released me.

"It wasn't a fun ride, but the real issue was the surprise guest at the police station. Guess who's been boinking Heather for years?" Not waiting for an answer, I filled him in on Simon's infidelity.

"Do you want me to beat him up?" Daniel asked. "I haven't done that for years, not since I was six, but I'd be happy to kick his butt."

"I appreciated it when you did it, and that boy deserved it for stealing my Barbie doll. But it was bad enough when you got suspended from school. Knowing how quick Simon was to hire a lawyer, you'd probably get sued. Besides, I've got bigger problems than Simon." I sank down on the bed, which housekeeping had made pin-straight again.

Daniel sat in the desk chair and swiveled around to face me. "You mean that you're now under suspicion for murder? I noticed you skimmed over the fact that they confirmed it was cyanide. And I'm so thankful you didn't try the soup."

"Me too. But the cyanide being in the entire pot will devastate Benjy. He'll be under suspicion too."

"You really think you're under suspicion?"

"I already am. Detective Preston kept saying how it was convenient that I delayed tasting the soup."

"I wasn't there, but I assume you lifted the spoon and inhaled deeply first." Daniel laughed. "You *always* do that. Even before you went to culinary school. It used to drive me nuts because you took so long to smell, taste, and eat your food. I had to wait forever until you were done before I had seconds."

"That wasn't my rule." Due to mostly absent parents, I'd been the cook for the family and had many rules, but that wasn't one of them.

"No, but I felt guilty if I ate more before you did since you did all the work."

A sharp knock at the door startled me. When I opened it, I knew immediately this wouldn't be good. Detective Preston and a few other police officers stood behind an uncomfortable-looking bearded man. The man, whom I recognized as the front desk manager, cleared his throat.

"Hello, I am Howard Cooke, the manager on duty." His soft Texas drawl did not fit the gravity of this situation. "I apologize for intruding, but these police officers have a search warrant for your room." He glanced unhappily at Detective Preston. "The hotel does apologize for the inconvenience."

Preston stepped forward, nudging the manager aside. "You're allowed to stay in the room if you so choose, but we'll be faster if we can just get in and out." He handed me the papers. "You'll see this warrant covers your hotel room, luggage, and any electronic devices other than your cell phone. It should take us about an hour to search, and then you may return to your room. We'll give you a receipt for anything we take to the station."

Preston didn't apologize for the inconvenience.

I thought being served with divorce papers was the lowest part of my life. Being served with a search warrant topped that. I stepped out of my own hotel room and watched as a platoon of police and what I assumed were evidence techs swarmed in. One officer maintained a watchful stance in the hallway, casting a suspicious gaze at Daniel and me, perhaps including Howard in the mix. Overwhelmed with disbelief, I closed my eyes, trying to process what had happened to my life.

Howard spoke up. "Ma'am, you're welcome to come downstairs and sit in our lobby. There's comfy furniture down there."

I opened my eyes and stared into his kind ones. "That's nice of you, but I can wait in my brother's room." Daniel nodded his agreement.

"Yes, ma'am." He looked like he wanted to apologize again, then pivoted toward the stairwell. I'm sure he was worried about how I would review the place. *Impeccable cleanliness and a staff that could rival the best, but the real highlight was the unexpected threat of a police room search. How thrilling it was to have my getaway disrupted by law enforcement rummaging through my belongings.*

I turned to Daniel. "Well, I'm glad I only brought my nice conservative underwear. Would hate to scandalize these young, innocent police officers."

Daniel put an arm around my shoulders. "Let's head back to my room. And contact a lawyer."

"Who should I call?" I asked when we were back in Daniel's room.

"Felicia Somebody is your lawyer, right?" Daniel asked.

"McKenzie, but she specializes in entertainment law. Negotiating contracts, protecting intellectual property, that kind of thing. Murder is probably not in her wheelhouse."

"Still, she might be able to recommend someone in this area."

"California and Texas aren't terribly close, Daniel."

"Just call her." When I started patting my pockets, searching for my phone, he sighed and glanced around. I'm glad the police hadn't included my cell in their warrant. Not that I had anything incriminating on the phone, but I'd be lost without it. Even though the cell itself was often lost.

Eventually, Daniel found my cell phone on the television stand and handed it to me.

When my call went to voicemail, it reminded me again of how far I had fallen. When I had been bringing in merchandising deals, television shows, and specials, Felicia would answer my phone call immediately. "Next idea?"

Daniel thought for a second, then raised his eyebrows. "April knows people who know people. Remember how she was able to find us someone to repair your car?"

He had a point. A quick call to April netted me a shocked gasp, a concerned question, and the name of a defense lawyer who practiced in Houston who was also a niece or cousin twice or three times removed. The follow-up call to Jessica Wong and the mention of April's name resulted in an appointment for early tomorrow—even though it was Sunday—and an admonishment not to talk to the police again without her present.

"So now what?" Daniel asked once I had set the appointment.

"I think we wait."

"Or..." He looked at me expectantly.

"Or?"

"The police seem to think you killed Heather. You know you didn't kill Heather. I know you didn't kill Heather. So, we find who *did* kill Heather."

"I've already done a search on the internet."

"Yes, but that was before you knew the poison was in the entire pot of soup. And sorry, sis, but I'm better with computers." He opened his laptop.

"How do we search for a killer if we don't know who the victim was supposed to be? I asked. "The poison could have been for Heather or Erica."

"Or you," Daniel pointed out.

"I'm trying not to actively think about that. I don't think anyone wants to kill me."

"Are you sure? Simon might benefit if you died before your divorce."

"I really don't have that much money left. Not worth killing for."

Daniel leaned back in his chair. "Since I've been handling your finances, I'm forced to agree. Would he have to pay you alimony?"

"I wouldn't take a dime from him." I took a deep breath to calm down and think. "But he's so greedy, he might be worried I'll be the same way."

"So Simon's a possibility. Or maybe I just like the idea of him behind bars." Daniel poised his fingers over his laptop keyboard. "Who else might have a motive to kill you?"

"I pissed off a lot of people during my drinking days. And my total collapse, losing my show, my restaurant, my sponsorship deals, meant that many people lost their jobs as well." I was still consumed by guilt at that thought.

"And you think one of them might have been gunning for you?" Daniel frowned. "I don't know, risking taking out two other judges just to get to you seems extreme. There are easier ways to kill you. Sorry."

"I think I'm thankful we've always had a good relationship." I sat on his bed, pondering. "Maybe it's someone who wanted to kill me and Heather, maybe someone who hates Gourmet Channel stars?" That seemed like a stretch, but people out there were crazy. "Have any other Gourmet Channel stars met unusual ends?"

Fingers flying, Daniel typed intently, then stared equally hard at the screen. After ten minutes, he shook his head. "Not that I can see. Who knew both of you?"

"Well, the mayor, obviously, having booked this gig. Then there's Benjy." I held up a hand to stop Daniel from even going there in his mind. "No way Benjy did it. Especially by poisoning his own soup. How dumb would that be?"

"Or how clever," Daniel said, his voice full of speculation. "As you said, most people would instantly eliminate him as a suspect for that very reason."

"He'd have nothing to gain and his restaurant—the one he named after his beloved niece—to lose."

"Fine, not Benjy," my brother said, a little pouty. "Then who?"

"I suppose both of us knew Skylar Brooks. I used to call her Super Fan. But now that I've talked to her, I just can't see her as someone capable of murder. Although…"

Daniel typed Skylar Brooks into a search bar. "Although?"

"Well, if she did decide to plan a murder, she'd probably be able to pull it off because she's obviously obsessed with details, research, and information." I looked over at my brother with a raised eyebrow. "You'd respect that since you do the same."

"I wouldn't call it obsessed, but yes, I do like those subjects. I can't find her on any social media platforms, at least not with her real name."

"I couldn't either. How about her dad? I don't know his first name, but he's a vascular surgeon and they live in Palo Alto. Does that help?"

He added that information to the search. "LinkedIn shows a Ronan Brooks, who is a vascular surgeon in Los Altos." He switched tabs. "This site shows a Ronan Brooks, who is related to Anna Brooks and Skylar Brooks. Includes their ages and probable worth of their house." He whistled. "That's an expensive house."

"She said her parents are well off. Still, I think they should let her go to culinary school."

"What?"

"Never mind. Just something she said." I told him about the more relevant parts of my conversation with Skylar.

Daniel leaned back in the desk chair and laced his fingers. "She might be handy for our investigation."

"We don't have an *investigation*, Daniel."

He leaned back forward. "Uh-huh. Well, our non-investigation has netted us very little information on Skylar Brooks." He glared at his computer, obviously annoyed that it had failed him.

"I'm guessing her parents don't want her visible on social media since they seem overprotective of her. I can't blame them, really. With her innocence, I could see someone targeting her."

"So, who else knew you both?"

I thought more. "I suppose the cameraman, um, Greg Wright, might have known us. He works for Gourmet Channel, so he might have worked with me or Heather before. I don't remember him. Not because I don't pay attention to the staff, but because, well, I don't remember much during the bad years. We need to come up with a better name for that time period."

"Do you have anyone you could contact to ask if Greg Wright was ever on the production staff of D-D-D?" He enunciated each D individually since shortening *Dinner, Drinks, and Decadence* to "triple D" was already used by another celebrity chef.

I searched for my phone and found it under Daniel's pillow. "I could ask my old director, but I feel really awkward texting him. What am I supposed to do, just say, 'Odd question, but did Greg Wright ever work on our production team, and do you think he'd want to kill me or Heather?'"

"How about just the first half?"

I texted my former director, despite the belief that he'd probably react the same way my entertainment lawyer had done. I was pleasantly surprised when my phone dinged, not even a minute later.

Not our show, no.

Nice way to put it. I started putting the phone back in my pocket when it dinged again. "He wants to know why. I'll tell him it's because after meeting him here, I was worried I might have insulted him if I hadn't recognized him." After I texted that, he again responded quickly.

Not sure. He's been with GC for a few years. Started off as a PA at Hacked *and then moved to* CC. *He was patient enough to put up with Heather, not to speak ill of the dead.*

So that information had already been passed around the Gourmet Channel staff. I wrote him back: *He worked on her show?*

Head cameraman.

I conveyed this information to my brother. "That's a pretty big jump. He was just a production assistant for *Hacked*, then was the head cameraman for *The Clean Cook*. That probably explains why he was here at this rinky-dink festival. Must have been covering Heather's activities, probably to include shots in a future episode."

"He worked for *Hacked*?" Daniel typed on the computer.

"Yeah. Do you think he was there when Heather and I competed? Or when Benjy did four months later?"

"According to his account on LinkedIn, he was on the show during those times. So you might have met him."

"And Heather and I did something to anger him badly enough to murder? That seems unlikely."

I jumped at the knock on the door. Detective Preston stood outside. "We're finished with your room. Here's a receipt for your laptop. We'll be in touch, so don't leave town."

I wasn't planning on it, but I wasn't going to talk to them without first discussing things with the lawyer.

When the door was shut, Daniel closed his eyes. I was about to ask if he was feeling okay when he sighed. "I want to ask how they were able to access your computer without asking for a password. But I'm very worried I know the answer."

I blushed. "Yes, I still have the password taped to the bottom. I kept forgetting the password."

"Jackie! I told you to fix that."

I escaped Daniel's lecture and retreated to my room. I was now uncomfortable in the space, knowing all my things had been touched, inspected. They hadn't left any obvious signs that they'd ransacked the room. My clothes were in the drawers or the closet, the empty suitcase was under the bed, which still looked nicely made, and everything seemed the same, other than my laptop not being on the desk. I wandered into the bathroom and nothing was out of place there either. Had they looked in here? Would my choice of shampoo give them clues as to whether or not I had killed Heather?

I was surprised when the hotel phone rang. Who would be calling that number?

"Hello, Ms. Norwood. This is Howard at the front desk. You have a gentleman in the lobby who would like to talk to you."

chapter thirteen

• • •

I MADE MY WAY DOWNSTAIRS, wondering about my mysterious gentleman caller. Hopefully, it wasn't Simon, not that he was a gentleman. It probably wasn't a police officer since Howard would have identified him as such.

When the elevator door opened, I saw Greg Wright standing at the desk, camera bag around his neck. I raised my eyebrows. Did he know Daniel and I were just talking about him? When he flashed me a grin, I guessed not.

"Hello, Jackie. I hope I'm not intruding."

"No, you're providing a nice distraction from worrying about Heather's death."

His smile dropped. "I get that. I'm actually here about that. The Gourmet Channel wants to produce a tribute to run after the next episode of *The Clean Cook*. We're interviewing those who knew her, getting some quotes from people. Since I'm here, I figured I'd ask for a quote from you."

I almost balked. What the hell nice thing could I say about her? Then I realized this was a way for me to spend time with Greg and ask him about his relationship with Heather. Plus, it was a good idea to get my face back on the Gourmet Channel. "I'd be happy to. Let me just freshen up. Where would you like to shoot the video?"

"I thought we'd do it from the crab festival tent to showcase her last event. Although sadly, the background won't have many people enjoying the festival since there weren't many attendees when I walked here. Mayor Tom is probably bummed. But the sunset should be a nice backdrop, even if we aren't facing west."

"Meet you there in ten?"

When he gave me a nod, I rushed upstairs and took out my makeup kit, glad the police hadn't confiscated my cosmetics. I refreshed my top knot and reapplied my foundation, focusing on covering up the dark circles under my eyes. I swept on some mascara, some shimmery, rose-colored lip gloss, and figured I was good to go. I wanted to look somber for this recording, not overly made-up. I also wanted to look healthier than in my drinking days.

I texted Daniel to let him know what I was doing and got an "okay" from him with a following "be careful." As I walked to the festival grounds, I worked up what positive things I wanted to say about Heather.

Greg had set up his camera on a tripod, aiming for a good view of the water with the yellow and orange-colored horizon rather than the festival. He was right. There weren't many people around. I counted maybe five on the Ferris wheel and perhaps three kids on the merry-go-round. And unlike at most fairs or festivals, I didn't see anyone eating or buying food. Probably too scared. I felt horrible for all the vendors.

Greg glanced up from his camera and gave a thumbs-up. "Looking good."

I fought a blush as I took my place next to the judging table. "Thanks. How long should this be?"

"Just a couple of minutes. I'll do subtitles to show your location, so you don't have to say it. I figured it would be a bit heavy-handed for you to say, 'I'm standing a few feet away from where Heather spent her last minutes.' So you can just say something nice about Heather. Or just make up something," Greg said, winking. "You're on in three... two...one."

I wiped the shocked look off my face and replaced it with a somber expression. "The culinary world lost a great chef this weekend." I let my eyes drift to the table where Heather had been sitting. "She was a big personality: immensely talented, driven, and creative. Her love of food was obvious in her cooking, and her love of her fans was obvious in the allergy-free recipes she worked so hard to perfect for them. My life will definitely never be the same." I paused, letting Greg know I was done.

"And cut," he said, stepping away from the camera. "Loved the last line. You didn't say how it would be different. I'm sure it'll be better."

I felt obligated to defend her. "That's not a nice thing to say."

He shrugged. "I worked with her. She wasn't the easiest to get along with. And she wasn't exactly shy about sharing her opinion about you. I figured there was no love lost between you."

I tilted my head. "Then why did you ask me to give a tribute? I assume you weren't planning on me telling the truth."

"Does anyone in this business tell the truth?" He scoffed. "But no, even though it might make for some good entertainment, I wasn't expecting you to badmouth her. You're here, on-site. How could we skip you?"

"I'm not exactly Ms. Popularity at Gourmet Channel."

"Which I'm aware of. But I believe in second chances, and it's just good TV. Your feud with Heather was fairly well-known in the industry, maybe even by fans. So you get to be gracious, spouting nice things about her."

"I didn't have a feud with her. She had a feud with me," I complained. "Forgive me for sounding like a twelve-year-old, but she started it. Complaining whenever I'd do better in a class than she did."

"Trust me, I've heard all about it." He folded his tripod and tucked it into his bag. "She was certain you cheated, said you slept with all the instructors."

I snorted, thinking back to the faculty staff. Ick. "I'm not that ambitious. There are some instructors you couldn't pay me enough to sleep with." I realized what he just said. "Wait, you've heard all about it?" While I had done my best, when I was healthy, to interact with production staff and treat them as equals, Heather seemed like the sort to look down on them. So if she was sharing these things with the production staff…

"Sure. Every staff party, she'd get drunk and start bashing you. Was pretty ironic, actually, when she'd slur her words complaining about your alcoholism. Kudos on beating that, by the way."

"Well, I didn't beat it, but thanks. It's a continual process. One day at a time, you know."

"I won't ask you out for drinks then. How about ice cream?" He raised one eyebrow.

I felt my stomach flutter. I tried to tell myself it was because this would give me more time to ask about Heather and her enemies. But hey, he was cute, and I was flattered. First, I needed to ask something important. "How old are you?"

"Twenty-six," he answered with a smirk.

"Okay." A four-year difference. Not too bad. Ignoring the fact that I hadn't yet had dinner, I smiled. "Ice cream sounds perfect."

"…it turned out that the new cameraman had no idea what he was doing. It was a low budget job and he'd gotten the job because he was the producer's nephew. When we reviewed the footage, we found he'd turned off the camera when we were supposed to be recording and turned it on when we were on break. We had tons of footage of the production crew talking to each other about the next scene. There were a few times when we heard him bad mouthing the other staff or saying crude things about the talent. The final footage was someone saying, 'Why is that light on' while looking at the camera."

I laughed, enjoying myself immensely. I think this was the most I'd laughed in years. "I don't think that ever happened on our set. But we did have one time when our dolly grip went off track and knocked over a steel rack with pots, pans, and other metal bowls. I waited until the set got quiet again and yelled, 'Ice cream man!'"

At his appreciative chuckle, my pleasure ramped even higher. The only thing better than a man who makes you laugh is one who laughs at your jokes. I needed to remember that since I had chosen poorly with my first husband. Simon laughed at me, not with me. There's a big difference."

Recalling my purpose here, I asked, "So Heather used to badmouth me? I really did nothing to her other than being better at some things than she was. And the restaurant world would have been big enough for both of us."

"She didn't like you. And it would get worse whenever she'd bring Si—her boyfriend—on set." He took a bite of his banana split.

I rolled my eyes. "She paraded my husband around? They weren't even discreet about it? Lovely."

"You know about their affair?" he asked cautiously.

"Just found out, actually. Detective Preston was kind enough to inform me while he was grilling me for murder."

"Good. I mean, not good. I just wondered when or if you'd found out."

I raised an eyebrow. "Did you worry that I'd killed her after finding out about the affair? No. I found out about it *after* she died." Then I scowled. "Wait, if you were worried I killed her, why the heck did you ask me out for ice cream?"

He grinned. "Well, you weren't preparing the ice cream. And you'll notice I kept my bowl near me. But honestly, based on your reputation and what I've seen on set, I didn't see you as the killer type."

"I suppose I'm glad to hear that. If you did think I was the killer, I wouldn't think much about your self-preservation instincts." I realized I shouldn't point fingers since I was meeting with him, and he was a potential suspect.

Greg swallowed another bite of his ice cream. "Now if you'd been the victim, I'd have easily been able to picture Heather killing you."

"She hated me that much?" I spun my empty sundae bowl. "Why?"

Greg shrugged. "Jealousy, I'd say. She'd always say things like she thinks she's prettier than me, a better cook than me, more talented than me."

"I never said any of those things. I don't know where she got those ideas."

"Well, you're definitely prettier than she was."

I felt my cheeks heating, shifted my eyes away, and watched the next person order ice cream. After a few moments, I turned back. "So, who could you picture murdering Heather?"

It was his turn to pause and study the customers. "Good question. She wasn't well-liked by the staff. She's a talented chef, don't get me wrong. But she treated anyone that wasn't, well, her, as inferior. She'd throw shade about other chefs. Talk badly about them. And not just the casual trash talk you chefs throw around. She meant it. Do you remember the *Hacked* episode you were both on?"

I squirmed in my seat. "No, actually."

"Oh, right. Well, you beat her handily, even with the drinking issue. But the two of you were leagues above the other two contestants, who were hacked in the first and second rounds. And Heather was mean to them. Especially to Sofia. She was so harsh to Sofia that she made her cry during the competition. The producer felt sorry for Sofia, so he edited some of it out, even though the director wanted to keep it in for the drama."

"Sofia?"

"Sofia Delgado. Creator of today's winning crab cake?"

I bit my lip. "I hadn't realized I'd competed against her. I never watched that episode, even knowing I won, because I knew I behaved badly."

Greg shrugged one shoulder. "It wasn't your best behavior. We had to edit many of your scenes too."

"I'm so sorry." I thought for a moment. "Do you think Sofia could have a motive?"

Again, that one-shouldered shrug. "I think anyone could have a motive to kill someone like Heather. There was one *The Clean Cook* episode where she advised those with allergies to be extremely careful about which restaurants they choose. She mentioned how she and a friend conducted an experiment and went to various restaurants, requesting no mushrooms due to allergies. Then they'd inspect the food, even take leftovers to a laboratory to test for traces of mushrooms. She said only one out of five restaurants she tested managed to have a mushroom-free dish. That's fine and good television, but while she didn't quite name the restaurants in question, she had taken video inside them, and the places could be easily identified. I'd think a chef or owner might be angry at that."

"Do you know the restaurants?"

"I wasn't the cameraman for those scenes, so I don't know. But the good restaurant was from a well-known restaurant chain in San Francisco. Don't remember which one. I forgot the bad restaurants."

"What episode is that?"

"*A Cause for Concern*. Season one, episode four, I think. Maybe five."

It looked like I had a lot of screen time in my future.

chapter fourteen
. . .

AFTER SAYING GOODBYE TO GREG, I hurried back to my hotel, ready to watch some videos on my laptop. That was when I remembered I didn't have a laptop. I stopped at the same bench where I had overheard the mayor and his wife and texted my brother.

Cue up my Hacked *episode. I wanna watch. Evidently, Sofia was on it, and Heather was mean to her.*

I know. I watched that episode since my sister was in it. Heather was harsh.

Can you also find the CC episode: A Cause for Concern? She panned some restaurants.

As I lowered my phone, I noticed a figure sitting on a different bench, staring at the water. Although it was odd to see him in jeans and a T-shirt rather than chef's whites, I recognized him. "You okay, Benjy?"

He didn't look up. "The entire pot was laced with cyanide."

I dropped down next to him and took his hand. "I know."

"*My* soup was poisoned. I'm under suspicion of murder."

"If it makes you feel better, so am I. Have they searched your room?"

He nodded. "Yup. And my van and the storage area they've

provided for us here." When he finally looked up, his eyes were fierce. "They aren't going to find cyanide. It's really not an ingredient I choose to use in my cooking."

"Me neither. It's too expensive, and there's no return on investment."

He snorted and ran a hand over his head. "Thanks, Jackie. I needed that." He took a slow, deliberate breath. "First, I still can't believe Heather is dead. I can't say I've interacted with her often since CIA, but I saw her at some competitions, a few festivals. And she sent flowers to Kimi when she was going through all her chemotherapy treatments."

"Sorry I didn't do the same."

He waved that away. "You didn't know about it. We both were deliberately ignoring each other at the time."

"Thanks to Heather."

"Yes, which Detective Preston keeps reminding me could go to motive. Are you getting the same play?"

"Yup." I leaned back on the bench. "And I have another potential motive. Guess who Heather's latest boy toy is?"

"Her cameraman?"

"Greg? Why would you think that?" I considered it. I hoped not. "Simon Levenson. *My* current husband, although I'm working on remedying that."

Benjy let out a low whistle. "I'm trying not to take comfort in the fact that you have a stronger motive than I do."

"Maybe you should join our investigation team."

"Your *what?*"

"Oh, Daniel has this crazy idea that since the cops are looking at me —and I didn't do it—we should do our own investigation to find the guilty party."

"In the past, I would have said he's insane. But I've never been a murder suspect before. Maybe it's not a bad idea."

I slumped against the bench. "Maybe. Obviously, they're looking at me. Hard. And it sounds like they're looking at you."

"They are." He threw his hands up in the air. "Fine, I'll join your investigation team. What's my assignment?"

"Right now, we're just pooling information." I sat up and turned to face him. "Okay, all marbles on the table. Let's be completely truthful."

"I've always been completely truthful." His gaze didn't break from mine.

I squirmed in my seat. "Okay, you're answering the first question I had for you. You never cheated on me with Heather, right?"

"I didn't. Now my turn to ask a question. Why the hell did you think I had?"

"I caught her talking to somebody about how amazing you were in bed. Then she noticed me, blushed, and scampered away. I still thought she was full of it. Then I went to your room, and it smelled like her perfume."

"Wait. I remember that day. I wondered why my room smelled like a funeral home and thought maybe my roommate had used a new cleaning product." He stared out at the waves for a while. "Okay, I get why you believed her. I still wish you had believed me when I said I hadn't."

"Me too, Benjy. Me too." We sat in silence for a while, staring at the waves. "So, did you kill her?"

He laughed and shook his head. "No. Did you?"

"No. Did you put cyanide in the soup to try and kill me?"

"Again, no. And before you ask, no, I wasn't trying to kill Erica either. Did you put cyanide in the soup to kill Heather and ruin me?"

"Nope. Now that we've settled that, can we head to Daniel's room? He's got a few episodes cued up on his computer."

I explained to Benjy what Greg had shared as we walked back to Daniel's room. I knocked on my brother's door.

"I've brought another investigator," I explained. "Considering he's currently on the suspect list as well." Daniel didn't say a word, but I knew my brother. "And he's not the killer."

He nodded but still didn't let us in.

I continued. "And he never cheated on me."

He stepped back from the doorway. As we entered, I noticed changes he had made for Investigation Room Central. He'd connected his laptop to the hotel television so we'd all be able to watch the show. I didn't feel comfortable lying on the bed with Benjy, and there was only the desk chair, so I slid down the edge of the bed and sat on the floor. Daniel got bottles of water from the mini-fridge, passed them around, then stretched out on his bed. That left the chair for Benjy. I was surprised when he chose to sit next to me.

After watching the episode, I took a sip of water. "I have to admit, if I was Sofia, I'd be ready to kill Heather after that episode. She was really, really rude."

"She was, but I just can't see Sofia killing anyone," Benjy said.

Daniel disagreed. "I think anyone could do it if pushed to a breaking point. Maybe something else was going on in her life. Or maybe Heather and Sofia connected somewhere else, away from *Hacked*. Anyone else we should think about?"

Benjy inclined his head. "There were people at the Culinary Institute who were jealous of you and Heather. The two of you were a force. First and second in each class."

"And you were often third," I said to Benjy.

"And I was often third. Still, I can't picture someone hating either of you enough to kill. Especially ten years afterward. But you know Veronica was a classmate, right?"

I raised my eyebrows. "Veronica Rossi, the contestant here?"

Benjy nodded. "Yes. She was Veronica Stewart back then."

"Ah, of the Stewart family empire. That explains how she has a chain of restaurants at her age. I vaguely remember Veronica. She didn't have that bright-orange hair then. Wait...Veronica wasn't involved in the Pastry Incident, was she?"

"The Pastry Inci—oh, you mean when you and Heather almost had a knockdown, drag-out fight?"

"There's no almost about it. Heather pushed me into someone's croquembouche." I turned to Daniel. "Croquembouche was the final exam for the baking and pastry skills class." At his blank look, I explained. "You saw croquembouche at our cousin's wedding. It's the tall tower of profiteroles."

"Oh, those cream puff things? They were delicious. How could balls of deliciousness cause a fight?"

"They didn't," I explained. "We were fighting about...umm...actually, I don't remember. I think she was being mean to someone. I defended the person, probably said some nasty words about Heather, and she pushed me. Right into another classmate's croquembouche. Knocked it on the ground. That tower had been perfect. Tall, completely symmetrical. Until I smooshed it."

"It was a mess," Benjy agreed. "I remember how devastated the student was. I can picture her, but I can't remember her name. Do you?"

"Mousy brown hair, right? Glasses?" I pondered. "I can't remember her name either."

"I don't remember graduating with her either."

We were silent for a minute, quiet enough that when my stomach growled, everyone heard it. "Sorry. Haven't had much to eat today other than bites of seven crab cakes and ice cream. I could definitely use some real food. Maybe we can order something?"

At that moment, we were surprised to hear a knock on the door. I looked at the alarm clock. "It's nine o'clock. Do you think it's the police?"

When Daniel opened the door, I registered the enticing smell of Chinese food before my brain realized whom I was seeing.

"April?" What was my AA sponsor doing here?

She stepped into the room, a large white bag in her hands. "I have brought food. I would love to say this is from my restaurants, but of course, if it had been, it would not have stayed warm on the flight." She set the bag down on Daniel's dresser. "But this place was highly recommended by my driver. Daniel, I ordered you your favorite *Zhīma jī*, sesame chicken. Jackie, I got you *Niu Mian Tang*, beef noodle soup." She looked over at Benjy and raised her eyebrows in my direction.

I shook myself from my surprised daze. "April Yao, this is Benjy Hayes. Benjy, this is April Yao, my AA sponsor, who is a crazy person who apparently flies to Texas on a whim."

"Ah, the ex-boyfriend and the chef who prepared the soup that killed Heather." She nodded sharply, went to Daniel's sink, and washed her hands. Before returning to the food, she checked herself in the mirror, tucked a few stray dark hairs back into her updo, and smoothed down her traveling outfit. I don't know how she did it, but her turquoise-colored silk pantsuit was still pristine and wrinkle-free.

"Benjy, I neither knew you were here nor knew your favorite, but I have purchased a number of different dishes. I have dumplings, both fried and steamed, salt and pepper pork, Chinese broccoli with oyster sauce, and steamed whitefish with scallions and garlic."

I shook my head. Typical April. There was a reason I had gained weight after finishing rehab. "Did you really just buy a last-minute ticket after talking to me today?"

"I did. As your sponsor, I support your sobriety efforts. I felt, considering the severity of what is happening to you this weekend, that you needed in-person support in addition to a lawyer."

Honestly, I was glad she was here. I'd been too busy to be tempted, but I felt strengthened by her presence alone. At twenty-five years sober, she was an inspiration to me.

"And food," Benjy said, helping himself to a large helping of everything.

April beamed. He had just earned her approval. She was going to nag me silly about him. Not that I'd need to worry about that if I was in prison.

"We were about to watch an episode of *The Clean Cook*," I said. "Now we can eat and watch. We're trying to see if that episode might have led to her death."

April loaded a plate and handed it to me, along with the entire container of beef noodle soup. "Here. Eat. Which episode? Do you mean the one where she goes undercover and investigates allergen compliance at various restaurants? My restaurants were featured in that episode. Even though Little Dragon did well—after one lawsuit, we are extremely cautious about potential allergens—I still considered that episode an overstep. She had video and audio coverage. This is especially bad in California, where they are very protective of privacy."

Ten minutes later, I had to agree. "That's so obviously your restaurant, even though she has the hidden camera aimed at the floor. But your carpet is distinct with—surprise, surprise—little dragons on it. Anyone could guess it was your restaurant. And she showed a picture of the menu for the one restaurant chain that did poorly. You can even see the Pasta n' Boots logo, which is pretty recognizable." I thought the distinctive shape of Italy redone as a cowboy boot was clever. "I'm sure Veronica was upset to have her restaurant featured as the worst at allergy awareness."

Daniel glanced up from his laptop. "Just confirmed it is the menu from Pasta n' Boots."

"How many restaurants does Veronica have?" Benjy asked around a mouthful of Chinese broccoli.

After a few clicks, Daniel answered. "Seven. Four in California, one in Nevada—Las Vegas, of course—and three in Texas."

"Must be nice to have that many restaurants," I commented, stabbing a dumpling with my chopsticks. When April raised an eyebrow, I blushed. "Sorry, April. Your situation is different. You built your empire yourself. You didn't have your parents bankroll one." When she continued to glare at me, glancing down pointedly at the food, I unspeared the dumpling and used the chopsticks correctly to grab it. She'd taught me that using chopsticks to stab food was verboten in China. Or whatever verboten was in Mandarin.

"I don't think I'd want a chain," Benjy said. "Consistency is good, on one hand, but it really limits creativity and spontaneity. Plus, you can't oversee them all equally to make certain they are up to your standards."

"You can use your specials for creativity and spontaneity," April disagreed. "And you make certain you have chefs you can trust and that you train well."

Benjy shook his head. "Yes, but—"

"Okay, chefs," my brother interrupted. "I understand this is an important question to you all, but can we get back to the idea of murder?"

I smiled at my brother to thank him for keeping us focused.

"Although," Daniel said, sitting straight and pausing importantly. "I was thinking. We keep wondering who the victim was supposed to be. Perhaps it wasn't aimed at a specific person. Perhaps someone at the crab processing plant added cyanide to a batch of crab, and then Benjy used that."

We all stared at him.

Benjy recovered first. "That would be horrible if someone did that,

Daniel. But, well, I didn't start with processed crab. I started with actual, living crabs."

"Oh." Daniel looked disappointed.

I quickly launched into a different tack to take attention away from my brother. "So we have a motive for Veronica because Heather panned her restaurant's allergy control. We have a motive for Sofia because Heather was horrid to her."

"What about the third judge?" April asked.

"As a victim?" I asked. "When I thought the poison was just in one specific soup bowl, I thought she might be the potential victim. I thought the mayor was trying to kill her, for whatever reason a man wants to kill his wife. I still wonder about that."

April waggled her finger. "No. Not as a victim. As the killer."

"Erica?" I gave it careful consideration. "She's so mousy and meek, but aren't those always the serial killers where all the neighbors act surprised? I don't know. I can't think of a motive for her to kill Heather…or me. Plus, with the poison in the soup, she was risking her own life as well or risking people noticing her not tasting the food. No, I still think she was the target."

"You still think the mayor wanted to kill his wife?" Benjy asked. "Why?"

"Who knows why spouses want to kill each other?" I responded. "Maybe he wants to upgrade to a new wife, but she doesn't believe in divorce. Maybe he took out a huge life insurance policy on her."

"But why here? Now?" Benjy asked. "He's so hyped about this festival. Why would he ruin it with a murder?"

I shrugged. "Maybe he thinks the police won't suspect him at his own festival."

"Fine. Let's investigate him," Daniel said, turning to his keyboard.

"I already looked him up online. Maybe we should do something more active."

Keeping his focus on his computer, my brother continued typing. "Like what? Break into Town Hall or something?"

"Umm…yes, actually." I watched as three heads swiveled sharply in my direction.

"And you call me crazy?" April threw her hands in the air.

"You can't be serious," Benjy said.

"I might be. After all, I can't just look up stuff about the mayor online because *the police took my computer*. Benjy and I are both currently under suspicion of murder. And while Detective Preston seems competent, and I have it on good authority that Texas police have a higher-than-average solve rate, I really don't feel like putting my freedom, or Benjy's, solely in his hands."

"Okay, James Bond," Daniel said. "Tell me, how will you get into Town Hall? Rappel from the ceiling like *Mission Impossible?*"

"You're mixing up your movies. And getting in is the least of our problems." I put my hands on my hips. "If you think my security awareness is bad, you should see his. I know the password to get into the building after watching over Erica's shoulder. And the code was hard not to notice since it was one-two-three-four."

I thought Daniel's face palm might leave a permanent scar. "Next, you're going to say he has his computer password, which is probably Password1234, is under his keyboard."

"Oh, I do that." April blushed. "My employees make fun of me for it, but I can not remember all those numbers, letters, and symbols."

"See, it's not just me," I said, staring at my brother.

"What if his office is locked?" Benjy asked.

"He doesn't like keys, Erica said." I glanced around the room, saw everyone was still unconvinced. I fell back on Daniel's bed. "Okay, maybe it's a bad idea. But I just feel like I have to *do* something. Not just peck at a computer. No offense, Daniel."

"None taken." He turned back to his computer. "And I get why you want to do more, but let's not risk our livelihoods, okay?"

"If I'm in prison, or if Benjy is in prison, that'll ruin our livelihoods too."

"Let's trust the police to do their job," April said. "You just turned your life around. We do not want you to do a U-turn and head to prison."

I hated that they were right. But still...

chapter fifteen
. . .

IT WAS a struggle to wake up the next morning since we'd spent several hours researching our suspects.

The most damning thing we'd found out about the mayor was that in college, he'd been a member of the College Republicans, the College Democrats, and the Libertarians of Rice University. Covered all his bases, I suppose.

We'd also hunted for information on Veronica Rossi and Sofia Delgado, but other than a number of articles about the Pasta n' Boots franchise, and one blog post about how Sofia's restaurant was a hidden gem, we didn't find out anything we didn't already know.

I dressed in gray yoga pants and a T-shirt, laced up my running shoes, grabbed a ball cap, and headed toward the door. Glancing in the mirror, I realized my shirt said, "Don't mess with the chef. We chop things into little pieces." While usually funny, it was probably not a good idea when I was already under suspicion of murder. I quickly found a plain red T-shirt.

I picked the same route Erica had shown me yesterday. The water views were amazing and, more importantly, calming, something I totally needed that morning.

It was odd seeing the festival area so quiet. The rides were off—was there anything more spooky than a carousel standing still? I swear the plastic horses stared at me as I ran by, eyes following. I shook off the creepy feeling and kept running.

The area might have been too quiet and devoid of people, but it did smell delicious. I followed my nose to the chefs' preparation area.

"You're up early," I said to Benjy, who had his food truck window open as he worked.

"Couldn't sleep, so I decided to put my energy to good use." He turned, lifted a basket from the deep fryer, and dropped something onto a plate with parchment paper. "Try this." He handed the plate out the window, then a fork.

Since I could see steam actively rising from the plate, I held off tasting it until it cooled down. I raised it up to eye level, checking out the form. "A croquette?" I asked.

Benjy nodded. We'd often played this game in culinary school: just given something with no information, and we had to identify the ingredients.

"It's beautifully cooked." It was. The outside was flawless: a deep brown, crisp, and even. I started singing "Good King Wenceslas" in my head. I used the fork to cut through the crust. "Listen to that," I said, admiring the crackling noise it made. Inside, it was warm, creamy, and gooey. No songs for those adjectives. Inspecting the inside, the crab was obviously the main ingredient, and it was packed full of that sweet goodness. I could also see bright chunks of yellow. "Corn?"

Again, he nodded. I speared half of the croquette and took a bite. Closing my eyes in appreciation, I savored the bite. "Delicious. The corn and the crab are so sweet and the mashed potatoes create a creamy effect with no cream. The panko provided a perfect texture and crunch. Your competitors are going to have their work cut out for them." I smiled at him. "Talking about work, I've got a workout ahead of me." I popped the last half of the croquette into my mouth and ran off.

Running down to the pier, I admired the day. Unlike yesterday, today was beautiful. Sunny, warm with breezes coming in from the gulf, and just a lovely day. I watched pelicans fly low over the water and observed dolphins frolicking in the surf. I loved living in California, loved my mountain view, but you couldn't beat water for calming scenery.

I kept running down the boardwalk, thinking, unfortunately, about murder. I still felt frustrated that we hadn't done more last night than online research. While I trusted the police to find the truth, it was taking too long for my comfort level.

The day was quiet, so I could hear the waves, the seagulls, the pumping of my own heart, and the rhythmic sound of my feet hitting the boards. I concentrated on my breathing, using techniques I was taught at rehab. Exhale the bad juju, inhale in fresh air, fresh start. The endorphins were kicking in too, so for the first time since Friday evening when I saw Heather, I actually felt good, strong.

After passing by all the shops—I really did need to come back when the stores were open—I left the boardwalk and prepared to cross the road to the park. I glanced around. I could see a few vehicles in the distance on Main Street, in addition to a couple of cars and pickup trucks parked on the side of the road.

I stepped off the curb and into the street. Since I was tuned into the sounds around me, I heard the revving of an engine. The peeling of tires had me jerking my head to the right, just in time to see a white pickup truck with tinted windows barreling toward me.

They say your whole life flashes before your eyes in moments of peril. I'm not sure how true that is. I did have some memories of delicious meals I'd enjoyed: that butter-poached lobster in Maine, the wagyu beef tenderloin in Japan, the regret that I had never tried fugu. But there wasn't much time to think about that. My main thought was to get the heck out of the way of this maniac.

I dove onto the pavement, squeezing in between two cars. The truck barely missed me and grazed the back of one of the cars, pushing it forward a couple of inches. I lay on the ground for a moment, the wind knocked out of me.

"Jackie, are you okay?"

I was surprised when Daniel crouched next to me. I rolled over, sat up, and stared at my torn-up hands. I flexed everything and focused on my body to feel if anything hurt. "I'm mostly okay. Just some scrapes and bruises, I think."

With Daniel's help, I gingerly stood. The truck was gone from my sight. "What the hell was that person's problem? They must have been in quite a hurry."

Daniel raised an eyebrow at me. "I think they were aiming for you, Jackie."

My heart skipped a beat. "What? No way. Why would someone do that?"

"Maybe because they didn't succeed on Friday? Or maybe because we're trying to find Heather's real murderer? Maybe because they think if they take you out, you'll get the blame?"

"Did you get their license plate?"

Daniel shook his head. "There wasn't one. Or it was covered in mud. But I checked as I ran out to you. Was there a front license plate?"

I closed my eyes and tried to picture it. "All I can remember is that huge grill on the truck heading right for me." I took some shallow breaths. "You think they were trying to kill me?"

"That would be my guess. We need to call the police." He pulled out his phone and called the emergency line. When they asked if I needed an ambulance, I adamantly shook my head no.

"No, we don't need medical assistance," Daniel said. "Just the police."

I was glad Officer Short was not the responding officer. Instead, Officer Tall—I forgot his actual name—showed up, took down the details, and contacted Detective Preston. He pulled up a few minutes later in an unmarked vehicle, wearing an unremarkable brown suit.

"I'll take over, Officer Mallory," he said as he approached. The officer nodded and got back into his vehicle.

Detective Preston raised an eyebrow and pointed toward a nearby park bench. "So, you reported that someone tried to run you down?"

I saw Daniel grit his teeth at the disbelief in Preston's voice. "Either that or you have really bad drivers in this town." I walked over to the bench.

"And your brother was a witness? Someone tried this while you were out running with your brother?" Preston glanced over at Daniel's attire: jeans and a green polo. "That doesn't quite look like workout gear."

Daniel narrowed his eyes. "I wasn't out running. I don't run unless someone is chasing me. But I know Jackie's routine, know she usually leaves around seven a.m. and runs for about an hour. I figured I'd join her for the cool down. You can check with the hotel front desk or hotel cameras, but I left the hotel only ten minutes ago."

"Did you leave at seven, Ms. Norwood?"

I nodded.

"You were returning to the hotel when this incident took place?"

"Almost. I was about halfway. I stopped by the festival and chatted with Benjy." I watched as both men reacted to that statement. "He was preparing a potential entry for today. I sampled it."

"Seems like a rather unfair advantage," Preston said.

"That I got to taste it early? I don't see how. I'm going to judge it based on how it tastes this afternoon, not this morning."

"Fine. I'm not concerned with you colluding with Benjy unless it applies to my murder case. What was your route after that?"

"I ran down and back up the pier, checked out the scenery, then ran down the boardwalk and was about to cross into the park."

"And you forgot to look both ways before you crossed the road?"

As Daniel prepared to respond, most likely with harsh words, I quickly gave him a settle-down gesture. "I *did* look. There were only parked vehicles. Including the white truck that almost hit me. Once I stepped into the road, I heard the revving of an engine and the squealing of tires."

"Did you see the driver?"

"No. I was focused on the two tons of truck heading straight for me."

"Mr. Norwood?"

Daniel shook his head. "The windows were tinted. It was a white Dodge Ram. At least it started out its life as a white one. It was filthy and had damage to its front and back bumpers."

"Maybe I wasn't the first human it aimed for," I muttered.

"License plates?" Detective Preston asked. I felt mollified that he had at last pulled out a notebook and pen. Maybe he was finally believing us.

"Nothing on the front," I said. "And Daniel said there weren't any plates on the back." I looked over at Preston. "Are front plates required in Texas?"

He nodded. "Front and back. Not that we enforce missing front plates unless there are other issues. But missing both plates is illegal." He stood and walked over to the street. "Where did the truck come from?" When I started to stand, he held up a hand. "Just stay there. Where did it start?"

I could see across the street from where I was. "Behind the green car on the opposite side."

"The Toyota Prius?"

"Behind the green car," I repeated. "I don't know car brands."

"Makes or models," Daniel corrected.

"That too."

Preston pulled out his cell phone and swiftly captured a series of photos. "I can see tire marks here. Looks fresh. Were they here before?"

I shrugged. "I didn't examine the road. I was only worried about moving vehicles. Not having seen any, I thought it was safe to cross."

He lowered the phone in his hand and started typing. "I'm requesting that the Forensic Science Unit process the scene." He turned around and faced me. "Now, Ms. Norwood, I'm going to need you to come down to headquarters."

"To talk about almost getting run over?" I asked, suspicious.

"No. To talk about what we found on your computer."

"What? There's nothing on my computer." I stood, grateful that nothing hurt when I did so.

"Are you certain of that?" Detective Preston asked.

"She's not talking to you without her lawyer," Daniel said. He checked his watch. "She's supposed to be here in a half hour anyway."

I glanced down at my outfit. I didn't want to wear sweaty workout clothes to an interview. Interrogation. Or for a potential mugshot. "May I shower and change?"

"And treat her injuries," Daniel added.

Preston gave me a long, thorough look. "You may. I'll see you and your lawyer at police headquarters at nine a.m., or we will find you and bring you in."

"I'll be there."

It was awkward to meet my new lawyer, and after giving her a synopsis of Heather's death, immediately ask her to accompany me to the police station. But Jessica Wong won my confidence by accepting that news calmly.

"He said he wants to discuss the contents of your laptop?" Jessica asked as we, along with Daniel, got into her car. "What could they have found on it?"

I shrugged. "I have no idea. I use it for recipe creation, information about my former restaurant, checking social media. That's it."

She stared at me solemnly. "Porn?"

"I don't want to know," Daniel muttered.

"Nope. Not even that."

"Have you searched for anything related to the case? Heather's whereabouts? Watched her television program?"

I started to shake my head, then reconsidered. Then shook my head. "No. Not even that. I watched her show on my television, but never on my laptop."

"Have you researched ways to kill people?"

"I've imagined many ways but never actually researched it."

I heard Daniel groan from the backseat.

Jessica glanced over at me. "Let's leave off that first part, okay?"

She asked a number of other rapid-fire questions as she navigated the small-town roads.

"Are you just preparing me for being interrogated by the police?" I protested.

Jessica inclined her head, sending her long dark hair spilling over one shoulder. "Precisely. Plus, I need to be prepared as well. You will say nothing unless I approve."

I sat there, waiting.

Jessica rolled her eyes. "You may speak now. When we are in an interview, please don't say anything unless I approve."

"Sorry. Sarcasm is my normal fallback to get through situations. And I've never been in this situation."

She patted my knee. "I have. You can trust me."

Thankful that I had Jessica and Preston had trusted me enough to let me come in on my own, I checked in at the front desk. Officer Short came out to bring us back to the interview room, one I was way too familiar with at this point. We dropped Daniel off in the waiting room, where I first saw Simon. I clenched my teeth. Cheating jerk.

Deciding that thinking about Simon and, therefore, Heather in a negative way was not the right frame of mind when being interviewed for murder, I turned my thoughts to something more pleasant. I took a cue from my life-or-death memories and considered my favorite meals ever. Japan was probably my favorite culinary location, with many memories of fantastic creations. The salmon sashimi that tasted like salmon-flavored butter, the wagyu beef so tender it melted in my mouth, the yakitori we'd picked up at a street vendor. I frowned. I had taken that trip with Simon, and he had refused to eat anything from street vendors. His loss.

"Can you stop thinking about whatever you're thinking about?" Jessica hissed as we stepped into the interview room. "You have changed expressions five times, and you don't have anything like a poker face."

Doing my best not to get Lady Gaga's song stuck in my head, we sat on one side of the table. Officer Short excused himself from the room, leaving Jessica and me alone.

Knowing there were probably people watching us, I was careful with my words. "I was thinking about food."

"You look that orgasmically happy over food?" Jessica asked, then sighed. "I should have known. I've seen Aunt April do the same."

I laughed and lowered my head. "They're watching, right?"

She leaned on the table, covered her mouth with her hand. "And listening."

So we waited, without talking, for a good twenty minutes. The only thing I hated more than waiting was silence. I worked in kitchens. There was never a silent moment. It unnerved me, only hearing my own breathing.

After thirty minutes, I was almost ready to confess to killing Heather if it meant we could get out of that room or at least turn on a radio or something. Finally, Detective Preston walked in, carrying a folder and my laptop.

I stared at my computer, wondering what he'd found that would be incriminating. I really couldn't think of anything. The worst thing I had done on that computer was look up a recipe for deep-fried bacon. And that was mostly just dangerous for my cholesterol level.

Detective Preston sat, took a deep breath, and stared at me. Once again, the silence drew on. I almost talked, but Jessica poked me.

"Since you have already inconvenienced my client by seizing her property and now insisting on her presence here, it would probably be for the best if you actually talked," Jessica said.

Sarcasm worked for her as well, I saw.

"Fine then," Preston said. "Let's not waste time. Ms. Norwood, could you explain why your search history includes sites that discuss cyanide poisoning?"

chapter sixteen

. . .

UNLIKE ME, Jessica had a poker face. She didn't react other than a slow turn in my direction. "Can you shed light on this?"

I blinked. "I already explained to them about this." Jessica nodded, so I assumed that meant I could talk. "After I explained Heather's symptoms to Daniel, he suggested that perhaps it was cyanide poisoning. I looked up that information on my phone."

"We're not talking about a recent search, Ms. Norwood. We're talking about an extensive search, months ago, covering information about effects, doses, efficacy, how long it will take, and how one can acquire cyanide."

I squinted at him in confusion. "I didn't research that much at all."

"It wasn't a phone search either. It took place on your laptop, beginning on February seventh of this year and continuing until March fifth."

He looked satisfied with himself. I'm sure he was pleased, his handcuffs at the ready. Those facts did make me look guilty. Like a cold-blooded killer. But I knew something he didn't.

I smiled. "Well, there are two chronological issues with that."

Jessica glanced over.

This time, I patted her knee. "First, I wasn't contacted about this festival until April. And I can't prove it, but I didn't know Heather was going to be here until I got here two days ago. But there's a much bigger issue."

"And that is?" he asked.

"I was not in possession of my laptop during those dates in question. I was in a rehab clinic, and they had restricted our access to outside contacts," I said smugly. As soon as those words were out of my mouth, I realized something major. Something bad. My stomach clenched.

"Then who had access to your laptop during this time?" Preston asked.

"Do I have to answer that question?" I asked Jessica.

"Give me a moment to talk to my client, please?" Jessica asked. When Preston left the room, she angled away from the one-way glass. "Am I going to be representing your brother now?"

When I nodded, she rolled her eyes.

———

Daniel and I exchanged places. He to the interrogation room, me to the waiting room. Where I did wait. And wonder. There was no way Daniel had killed Heather. First of all, he wasn't a killer. And he definitely wouldn't have risked my life poisoning an entire pot of soup just to take her out.

But admittedly, I had no freaking idea why he spent so much time and energy researching cyanide. On my computer, no less. He had his own. He'd been staying at my house while I was in rehab.

I just had to suffer through the waiting before I was able to learn the answers to these questions. I was relieved when Daniel came out of the interview on his own and without handcuffs. Jessica was beside him, looking concerned but not apprehensive. "Are you okay?" I asked him.

Daniel nodded and grabbed my hand. "Yes, but let's get out of here before anyone changes their mind. Jessica, let me take you out for lunch."

"Sure," she agreed. "After all, I got a two-for-one sale on clients. I won't even charge you for the lunch. We'll celebrate that neither of you is in jail."

"Was it close?" I asked as we exited the police building.

She shrugged. "Not terribly. What they had on both of you was purely circumstantial, with the cyanide search on your computer and your negative relationship with Heather. But I've seen people arrested on just circumstantial, so we should be thankful this detective didn't."

"I still don't understand that search history, Daniel. Why were you researching cyanide? And why on my computer?"

Daniel pivoted sharply, walking toward a barbecue restaurant. He pushed open the door. "Why don't we get something to eat. I'm famished." Finding a table—which wasn't a problem since it was barely eleven a.m.—he sat without waiting for an answer and picked up a menu.

I recognized a stall tactic when I saw one. But being the older sister, I didn't have to put up with it. "Daniel. Answer my questions."

He scowled at me. "What, now you're the police?" He turned to Jessica. "Am I required to answer her question?"

Jessica laughed and raised both hands in the air. "I'm not getting in the middle of this. I stayed away from family law for a reason."

Daniel sighed. "I was using your computer because my laptop's power supply kept overheating. While I was waiting for a new one to come—and it took forever—I used your laptop. It's not like you were super secure with your password. Or are." He glared.

"That's fine," I said. "Understandable. And now the first question?"

He squirmed in his seat. "So this is actually a good thing. But because we've been embroiled in this mystery, I thought I should wait until we weren't discussing real-life death and murder to tell you."

I stared at him.

"I've been..." He stopped, restarted. "You know how much I love to read mystery novels."

I nodded, hopefully encouragingly so.

He picked up a napkin and started shredding it. "And since I had so much free time while I was on leave to help you...I decided to write one."

"A mystery novel?" I asked in surprise.

"Yes."

Looking closely at my brother, I could see that below the worry about being interrogated, there was pride. And happiness. I smiled. "So that's why you were researching cyanide?"

"Exactly. And I'm really sorry my research led to you being suspected of murder. Truthfully, that was so long ago that I totally forgot I had done it until I was sitting in the waiting room, wondering what they could have found. I never even thought about my cyanide research because I eventually decided to go with *Phyllobates terribilis*. It's an alkaloid toxin from the Golden Poison Frog, considered by many to be the most poisonous and toxic animal in the world. One milligram of poison can kill twenty to thirty humans. Or two African Bull elephants."

Luckily, the waiter came over to take our order, so I didn't have to respond to Daniel's choice of poison. While I'd keep it in mind if I ever had to kill any African Bull elephants, I would think that something like that would be difficult to procure and use without poisoning yourself. But hey, he's the mystery author, not me, I suppose.

I wavered about whether I should order food since I had the tasting this evening. But I figured with all this stress, I'd burn off the calories before this evening.

After we ordered pulled pork sandwiches for Daniel and me and a brisket platter for Jessica, we continued the conversation.

"So, did the police accept that answer?" I asked.

"They did," Daniel said. "Especially since I was able to show them an email with a contract from a publishing company, proving I had been writing."

Now I was really impressed. "You managed to write a novel *and* get it published in"—I did the math—"three months?" It took way longer than that to write and publish a cookbook.

"It's not published yet," Daniel said. "I still need to sign the contract, and then they'll set a date. But when I took the call right before your tasting on Friday, that's who it was from."

"Your agent?" I asked.

He shook his head as he arranged and rearranged the plastic utensils. "No. I don't have an agent. The publisher contacted me directly."

That sounded fishy to me. I turned to Jessica. "Do you look at contracts too?"

"No. You'd want a contract lawyer or, even better, an entertainment lawyer to take a look at it. Before you sign it."

"I suppose I could ask Felicia McKenzie to take a—"

Jessica interrupted, "Hello. I need to point out to both of you that this should not be your highest priority."

"Right. We should be finding the true killer," Daniel said.

"What?" Jessica sat up straight in her seat. "No. You need to leave that to the police. I promise it won't endear you to them if you're interfering."

Daniel and I exchanged glances as the waiter brought our food.

"I saw that!" Jessica said after the staff had moved on. "Don't even think about it."

I picked up my pork sandwich. "If you were in our position, you would just let the police, who have already shown they suspect us—"

"And Benjy. The police suspect him too." Daniel interjected. "Her boyfriend," he added when Jessica raised an eyebrow.

"Ex-boyfriend," I clarified. "But since I know he didn't do it, I don't want him to go to prison either."

"I don't know," Jessica said as she picked up her fork and knife. "I have a number of ex-boyfriends I'd love to see in prison. Sadly, being a jerk is not a crime."

Daniel chewed thoughtfully, then swallowed. "There is one good thing that came from the interrogation."

"What is that?" I asked. "Besides finding this barbecue place? Their sauce is just the right balance of sweet, vinegary, and spicy."

"Yes, that. But we now know what type of cyanide was used."

"We do?" I mumbled over another mouthful of pork.

"Potassium cyanide. While the search history would have shown I researched all different types of cyanides, as well as other poisons, that's the only one they asked about. So most likely, Heather was killed with potassium cyanide."

"I have to agree with him," Jessica added. "They were very focused on that particular compound."

"What do you know about potassium cyanide?" I asked my brother.

"It's definitely not as powerful as *Phyllobates terribilis*. But you can kill twelve people using a single teaspoon of potassium cyanide. And it's somewhat easy to get. It's got a lot of uses, like in old-fashioned film developing, jewelry cleaning, and gold mining."

"Great," I said, rolling my eyes. "We just need to find a photographer gold miner who wants clean jewelry. No problem."

"I just mean that it's easy to acquire," Daniel defended. "It's also commonly used by people to commit suicide. Especially the Nazis at the end of World War II. And the whole Jonestown massacre was—"

I knew Daniel could spout this stuff for days, so I interrupted him. "Focus on information that can help us locate the killer. I doubt we're looking for a former Nazi or someone who drank the Kool-Aid. Does knowing it's potassium cyanide let us know when it was added to the soup?"

"It was actually Flavor Aid, not Kool-Aid," Daniel said, shaking his head. "Not sure why Kool-Aid gets the bad rep."

I inhaled slowly. "Really, really not important right now."

"I'm just saying," Daniel said. "And no. It doesn't help us know when it was added to the soup. Not really. It's colorless, so it wouldn't have affected the look of the soup. It does affect the taste of the soup, so I'm surprised Heather didn't notice. And as you've already noted, Jackie, it can smell like bitter almonds, but only for those with the genetic trait to sense that. Not all can."

"Yay, me," I said sarcastically.

Jessica leaned in and, unlike Daniel and me, spoke quietly. Perhaps we shouldn't be talking so casually about poison. "Don't I remember reading that cyanide is in apple seeds or something?"

That flashed me back to my childhood. "Right, there was a Trixie Belden book where one of the characters was affected by cyanide poisoning from eating apple seeds." I noticed Jessica's blank look. "You've never heard of Trixie Belden? She was like Nancy Drew but better. I used to love to read my mom's books."

"I remember that one too, Jackie," my brother said. "I think it was from eating whole apples in a Waldorf salad. I seem to recall that even then, you thought that person must have been a horrible chef, using whole apples instead of seeding them."

I laughed.

"But apple seeds," he continued, "almond shells, peach pits, all of those contain a substance that turns into hydrogen cyanide when digested. But Detective Preston was focused on potassium cyanide in our interview. That has to be the poison used."

I shuddered, realizing just how close I had been to death. Thank God that I, and also Erica, tended to savor the tasting moment rather than just dive in.

My phone beeped. "Speaking of Erica," I said. At Jessica and Daniel's confused looks, I realized I hadn't actually mentioned her aloud. "Never mind. She's texting me."

I read the text to them. "She says the mayor has hired additional guards for the festival and for tonight's tasting. I suppose I'm glad to hear that, but I'd much rather hear that the real killer has been caught. Take the heat off me, Benjy, and now you, Daniel."

He waved that away. "They don't really think I did it."

At that moment, Detective Preston walked into the restaurant. My hope that he was there for some brisket faded quickly as he walked toward us with somber determination.

"Daniel Norwood, we have a search warrant for your hotel room which will be carried out momentarily. We also ask that you, and your lawyer, come with us as we have further questions."

chapter seventeen
. . .

STANDING OUTSIDE THE RESTAURANT, I watched Jessica and Daniel as they trailed Detective Preston, keeping my eyes on them until they disappeared from sight. My stomach churned from the barbecue I'd just eaten.

When I turned around to head back to the hotel, my gaze landed on the last person I wanted to see, then or ever.

His scowl when he saw me demonstrated that the feeling was mutual and turned his face into an ugly mask. I can't believe I'd ever found this man attractive. Expensive polo shirts and khakis didn't cover up his personality.

"Did Daniel kill Heather?" Simon asked as he stalked toward me. "You couldn't even manage that on your own. You had to have your baby brother help you?"

"Of course he didn't kill her. Why would he have?"

"I don't know." Sarcasm dripped from every word as he leaned in, disrupting my personal space. "Because of the affair?"

"Which we didn't find out about until Detective Preston told me *after* Heather was dead." I crossed my arms in front of me. "And trust me, if I *had* found out about it beforehand, it's not Heather who would have been killed."

"That's what I told the police."

"You told *what* to the police?"

"That Daniel was a danger to me now. That I'd already been threatened by your brother." He paused. "He told me he'd kill me."

"Daniel did no such thing," I hissed out.

"He did. At our wedding reception, even. He said if I ever cheated on you, he'd kill me."

Realizing we were close to screaming at each other on a street full of cars and people, I grabbed his shirt and dragged him into the restaurant and back to our table full of half-finished meals. Still a public place, but the staff was probably already talking about my previous conversation with Jessica and Daniel.

I dragged a chair back. I wanted to shove him down, but he'd report that to the police too. "Sit and shut up. You're a moron, Simon. He didn't mean it. It's called hyperbole. Exaggeration, if hyperbole is too big a word for you."

He stared at me with brown eyes I once thought soulful but now saw as soulless. "That's what I thought too before Heather died."

"Neither Daniel nor I killed her, Simon. We had no idea she'd even be here."

"Please," Simon argued. "You totally baited her by telling her you'd be a judge here. You knew she'd be all over it once she heard that!"

"I did not. I didn't actually advertise this event at all. I don't have a PR person anymore to do my public relations, and I wanted to make certain this went well before talking about it." I'm not sure this qualified as "went well."

"She found out from someone," he insisted.

"Wasn't me. And wait, you're saying Heather came here deliberately to steal my glory? Stealing my husband wasn't enough?"

His nostrils flared as he blew out a breath. I realized that ever since my talk with Skylar, I was paying more attention to body language. "Never mind all that. We're talking about Daniel killing someone."

"He. Didn't. Kill. Anyone."

"The police think he did. They asked me all sorts of questions about him. What he did for a living, that sort of thing. Why he went on a sabbatical from his job. Whether he'd ever talked about writing."

They must have been checking into his alibi about researching cyanide for his novel. "What did you tell them?"

He shrugged angrily. "I told him I didn't know any of that. I thought he did something with computers before."

I sighed. I should have recognized the red flag that Simon never cared to learn about my family, my friends earlier. "He was a systems administrator for a security company."

He shrugged again. "Something with computers. And I admitted we hadn't talked since you went into rehab but that he probably went out on a sabbatical to take care of you. And collect a salary from the money you're hiding from me."

This was a major point of disagreement during our divorce proceedings. "There is no hidden money, Simon, I promise. I spent it all on legal fees, rehab, and the restaurant closing."

"I told the cops about that too. How you're delaying the divorce over money. That would also give you a reason to kill Heather."

"How would our divorce provide a motive?" I held off offering the fact that killing *him* would solve all these issues much faster.

"You didn't want her to have me or any of your money."

"Had I known, she could have had you. You're perfect for each other. And there's no money to be had. Even if there was, I don't do murder. Daniel doesn't do murder. And more importantly, he wouldn't have risked my death. The poison was in *all* the soup, Simon. Not just Heather's bowl. Which was originally Erica's bowl. Until Greg preferred hair colors—oh, never mind all that."

"What?" He looked as confused as I felt.

"Daniel didn't kill her. I didn't kill her."

"So who did?"

Throughout our unhealthy marriage, I had found sometimes a good defense was a good offense. I went on attack. "Maybe you did."

He slammed back in his chair in surprise. "Me. What for?"

"I don't know. Maybe you got tired of her. Lord knows she was annoying. And because you were mine, she wouldn't have wanted to give you up. You couldn't get rid of her. So you decided to kill her. And if you were lucky, you would have done a two-for-one deal if I'd died as well. And poor Erica would have been an innocent bystander."

"And how did I spike the soup when I was nowhere near the tent?"

"Hiding from me, were you?"

I could see Simon's hands clench before he answered. "Just waiting. Heather wanted to surprise you on Friday with her presence, and then on Saturday, we'd surprise you again with mine."

"Surprise is such a nice word, like it would be a pleasant experience. I think it's more she wanted to shock me. Or appall." And she succeeded on both, even from the grave.

"That was her intent, I admit. I didn't think it was a good idea."

"No, you wanted to wait to announce your relationship until the divorce was final."

"She was hoping this would encourage you to do a fast divorce." He slanted his eyes away.

Knowing Simon, knowing Heather, I made an educated guess. "Or encourage me back into drinking, right? Which you and your lawyer would then use to your advantage."

He blinked rapidly, a sure sign he was about to lie. "That wasn't our plan at all. We'd never purposefully do that."

"Even if that was your goal, too bad for you. I'm stronger than you think." With that, I stood up and stormed out the door.

———

On my way to the hotel, I thought about finding a place for a drink but reminded myself that I was stronger than *I* thought. Instead, I took a detour to see what was happening at the festival.

When I ended up in the competitors' area, I admitted to myself that what I wanted was to see Benjy. Luckily, he was in his food truck. I noted there was a guard stationed next to it, presumably to stop any tampering from outsiders…or from Benjy.

"Can you come out?" I asked. "Or am I interrupting some pivotal step in the process?"

"No, I'm just trying to perfect the croquette." He wiped his hands on a towel and disappeared from view. When he stepped out of the food truck, I told him everything that had happened that morning. I was grateful for all his reactions, including his disbelief that Daniel was a suspect. And I appreciated his worry over me. "Are you okay? Are the police doing anything about the attempt on your life?"

"They're more interested in proving my brother is guilty than finding out who tried to kill me. Besides, we didn't get the plate number, and I'm sure Texas has a ton of old white pickup trucks. I'm half convinced it was just a drunk driver or something."

Benjy looked less confident of that. I was about to reassure him when my attention was drawn elsewhere. "Oh look. There's Veronica at her booth. Now's our chance to see if she was the victim of Croquembouche-gate."

"Croquem—what? Oh, the Pastry Incident." Benjy shook his head but followed me to Veronica's cooking station.

"Hey, Veronica," I said casually.

"Hey, Usain Bolt." She smiled. "I saw you running after the dog yesterday. You're pretty fast."

"Not as fast as the dog was," I said. "But thankfully, Benjy outsmarted him."

"To the detriment of my knees," Benjy said. "It was worse than I thought, actually."

"He was a track star in high school. But he was reminded high school was a long time ago," I said, attempting a sequitur. "Just like culinary school was a long time ago."

Benjy's rolled eyes told me his opinion of my attempt at nonchalance. I kept going anyway. "I definitely have some fond memories of that time. And some regrets."

Veronica nodded. "Don't we all? But what would life be without some regrets?"

"True. But I still feel bad for that time when I destroyed that croquembouche tower." Channeling Skylar, I inspected her body language for any reaction. Her forehead wrinkled, but it looked like she was more flustered than furious.

Her brow then smoothed out. "Oh, I remember that. Your fight with Heather actually got physical, right? And you fell into someone's final pastry project?"

I didn't see any signs of long-simmering resentment. "She pushed me into it. While it was her fault, I still feel bad. Do you remember whose project it was?"

"It was a female," Veronica said slowly. "But I can't remember much after that." She laughed. "I wish you had knocked over mine. Mine was the Leaning Tower of Croquembouche. I could have used an excuse for why it looked so bad. Anyway, I need to finish up tonight's entrée. At least our odds of winning are going up." She gestured around her at the sparsely populated chef area.

I pondered as I walked away. "Could that be the motive? To force other chefs to leave so there's a better chance of winning?"

Benjy shook his head. "The prizes aren't worth that much. And if they had taken out all the judges by poisoning the entire pot of crab soup, then there wouldn't have been a prize to win. Interesting idea though. Perhaps a better idea than the Pastry Incident, which seems to be a red herring."

"Red herring croquembouche would be disgusting." I made a gagging noise, then considered. "Although, if you made it a savory cream puff, it might not be too bad. It's basically like your crab croquette, really."

"I'm not making a tower of them. What would I use to stick it together, caramel sauce? Hmm...." He furrowed his brow. I could almost see the gears turning in his head. "I need to go."

I smiled at his retreat. No doubt I'd be tasting a crab croquembouche tower this evening. It might be interesting. Fish sauce caramel had become pretty popular. Perhaps he'd incorporate a savory version of that.

I'd rather think about a crab caramel than about my poor brother being interrogated, maybe arrested.

Back in my room, I was barely there for two minutes before there was a quick knock at the door.

"I have been worried," April said, stepping into the room. "Jessica won't return my texts, you won't, Daniel won't."

I reached for my phone, noting the many texts from April. "Sorry, I turned it on silent when I was being interrogated. And then kept it off when it was Daniel's turn."

"Daniel's turn?"

I explained everything to her: the search on my computer for cyanide, the swap to Daniel being suspect number one, the police releasing him and then coming back for him, probably due to Simon snitching that Daniel had threatened him.

"That is ridiculous. Daniel would not hurt a fly." April said, rolling her eyes. "And he would not have risked you being a victim."

"Nor would he have been okay with Erica being an innocent bystander." I frowned. "I'm still not ready to rule out that the mayor is responsible."

April shook her head. "He is in charge. He is responsible for this, and anything that happens reflects on him. You do not poison your own well."

"You didn't mention not poisoning your own wife."

She snorted. "That, people do all the time. Or a more violent death. No one can bring out a murderous rage like a spouse." She crossed herself. "Unlike Ming, who was a perfect husband, God bless his soul."

"Amen." I didn't bother to explain that my reply was in response to her comment about murderous rages and spouses. I had never met Ming. He'd died fourteen years ago.

"We cannot do anything until we hear back from Jessica and Daniel. What are you wearing tonight?" April asked in a total non sequitur. "There will probably be a lot of cameras there. Show me your outfit."

I sighed but decided it was easier to obey. April Yao: AA sponsor, life coach, legal advice provider, and now fashion guru. I had to admit, she did have style. I had never seen her in casual clothes. When she wasn't wearing chef's whites or traditional Chinese garb, she was wearing sharply tailored suits. Even today, while she had no role other than to support me, she was wearing a gray suit set off by a lavender collared shirt.

"I'm not terribly colorful." I pulled beige capri pants and a matching jacket out of the suitcase.

She scowled. "You packed this wrong. It is horribly wrinkled. One moment." She left, presumably getting something from her room.

In a few minutes, she was back. At first, I thought she was carrying an iron and wondered why since my room already had one. All hotel rooms had one. But then I realized what it actually was. "You carry a garment steamer with you?"

"Of course. Traveling is no excuse to have wrinkles." She plugged the steamer in, arranged the clothes on a hanger, and hooked the hanger over the bathroom door. "What are you wearing under this?"

I raised an eyebrow. "What, you want to approve my underwear?"

"No. I mean, what shirt are you wearing under the suit jacket."

"I wasn't planning on one?"

She eyed the jacket, then turned the same beady eye on me. "No. That is too low-cut. And you need some color. Do you not have a colorful shirt?"

"I told you I wasn't colorful."

"I will be back again."

I knew she was heading back to her room to grab me one of her blouses. I wasn't certain I would fit into it. While we were both slim, she was six inches shorter than me.

At the knock at my door, I let her back in, unsurprised to see her holding a bright shirt. "The turquoise will set off your eyes. Put it on."

I hesitated slightly, wondering if she wanted me to strip right there or go to the bathroom. When she gave me an impatient look, I shrugged, stripped off the shirt I'd been wearing, and put on the turquoise shirt. April must have been very protective about my cleavage since the shirt was a high-neck sleeveless camisole. I slipped it on, not surprised when it was slightly too short.

"You will just need to leave the jacket buttoned then."

"No problem. That was my intention before. I hadn't planned on showing everyone my bra."

She tsked. "It is a very nice one, very delicate and flattering. But I agree that is not something everyone should see."

I picked up my cell phone, wondering what was happening with Daniel. Then, unable to stand still, I walked around my room, picking up the itinerary for the festival.

"Looks like I'm missing a meet-and-greet with a Texas senator. I'm sure the mayor is there, sucking up to him."

It was silent in the room for thirty seconds. "I'm sure the mayor is there," I repeated. "Erica would be there too. Town Hall is probably empty."

Our eyes met. "Jacqueline, I thought we talked you out of this last night."

"Last night, *I* was the suspect. Today, it's my little brother. The only one who stuck by me through rehab—before I met you, that is. The one who gave up his career for me."

April sighed and sat on my bed. "That does not mean giving up your freedom for him."

"It's two p.m." I ran over to my purse and grabbed my wallet. "If I get caught, I'll say I lost my driver's license on my run yesterday, that I thought I might have left it in the restroom. We can say the building was open."

April wavered. I could see it. "I suppose it would look less suspicious if you were discovered during the day than if you had done this last night. But I don't know…"

"We won't be discovered. But if we are, I'll admit that Erica used the code in front of me, and it was so easy to remember that I assumed everyone was free to use it to get in. Besides, I'm sure all the police are going to be providing security at the senator's event. I won't get caught."

The sigh was louder this time. "As your sponsor, I am supposed to talk you out of bad decisions." She took a deep breath. "But Daniel is a sweet boy, and these police officers are worrying me as well. I have enough money. I will be able to post bail if we are caught."

"We?" I asked.

"Two people can search faster. And it will add to your cover of you looking for your driver's license if you bring someone else. But…"

She paused, with a significant look my way.

"But?" I asked.

"You need to change again. That outfit is not appropriate for breaking in."

chapter eighteen
. . .

EVIDENTLY, all the cool burglars these days were wearing black, according to April. I thought it was too obvious, but it was easier to just change into dark leggings and a T-shirt than argue with her. April was, as usual, more elegantly attired in a black suit with subtle gold embroidery on the edges.

Luckily, Main Street was practically a ghost town. It seemed like anyone in town was at the festival, so there was no one on the street to watch our crazy antics. And since the area was mostly comprised of office buildings, I wasn't worried about nosy neighbors seeing two people dressed like cat burglars enter Town Hall on a Sunday.

I glanced around, confirming there were no obvious onlookers. Keeping my fingers crossed, I entered 1-2-3-4 into the silver keypad. The red light blinked once, then turned green. Sighing in relief, I opened the door, only to hear the loud beep-beep-beep of an alarm.

"Jacqueline!" April said.

"Relax. It's the same code." Another 1-2-3-4, followed by the Off button, and we were gifted with silence once more.

"Now what?" April asked anxiously. I wasn't certain a life of crime suited her.

"Now we go to the right. The restroom, by the way, is on the left."

"I might need it," April admitted. "I did not realize I would be this nervous." She raised her eyebrows. "That could also be our excuse. You can say we were walking around, and I needed to use the restroom. It was an emergency situation, you know how it is with old women, so you let me in, remembering the code."

"Not bad," I said. "I just wish we hadn't dressed up like ninjas then. It makes us look guiltier."

She scowled. "We can say it is in honor of Heather."

I rolled my eyes as we crept toward the office. Even though the building was empty, maybe because the building was empty, we tried to be quiet. I took a hand towel I had borrowed from my room and used that to open the door. As predicted, the mayor's office was not locked.

I put my hands up, blocking April from entering. "Wait." Taking out my phone, I snapped some photos of the office, of his desk setup. "This way, we can make certain we put everything back exactly as it was. Go ahead."

"That is very smart, Jacqueline."

And necessary. The desk, positioned at the center of the room, was strewn with an assortment of papers, folders, and pens. I hoped I could replicate it when we put the room back to rights. Across from the desk, a circular table with seating for four was likewise covered in paper, although these appeared to be in organized stacks. A file cabinet stood to the left, its second drawer slightly ajar. Framed photographs of the mayor adorned the walls.

I appreciated that the blinds behind the desk were drawn, allowing slender rays of sunlight to filter through but block the view of anyone walking outside. The soft light also revealed dust particles floating in the air.

I immediately slid behind the desk and started poking at the computer. Not surprisingly, it needed a password. I flipped over the keyboard.

"Is the password taped underneath?" April asked as she bypassed the desk on the way to the file cabinet.

"Not taped to it, but there is a sticky note under the keyboard with the code on it. But it's not Password1234, like Daniel figured. It's Crabs4Redding1234."

April laughed as she fully opened the second drawer. "So now what am I looking for?"

"A document titled, 'How to kill people with cyanide' would be great."

"I have not found that but here is a folder titled *First Annual Redding Beach Crab Festival*." She pulled it out and brought it over to the round table.

"There's nothing exciting here," she said after a moment. "Just logistic stuff. Contracts for the vendors, the guests, insurance policies. Your contract and Heather's. Nothing sticks out, other than the fact that Heather's contract to be a judge pays more than yours and is just four days after you signed."

"Which was April third, right?" I asked.

"You know the exact date?" April asked. "I am impressed with your memory."

"Don't be. I have the email from Mayor Tom to me where I emailed him the attached signed contract."

"You are in his email?" April stood up and hurried over, leaning over my shoulder.

"Yes. And talking about dates, I find it very interesting that two days after I agreed to participate, Heather emailed *him* to offer her services."

"How would she have known to do that?" April asked.

I mused for a moment, then scowled. "Probably from Simon. I told Simon, in a stupid effort to show I was rebuilding my career and we should reconcile. And he must have passed that info on to Heather." I held back a few choice words for my soon-to-be ex-husband.

April patted my shoulder, then pointed. "What is this email about life insurance?"

I clicked open the email from a well-known insurance company. "Interesting. Four months ago, he increased Erica's life insurance policy to two million dollars. I wonder if he did the same for himself."

I put the insurance company name in the search bar. "It looks like he did do that, at the same time. And what's this email?"

"Event cancellation insurance?" April asked. "What is that?"

"Thank you for choosing us for your insurance needs," I read aloud. "We are happy to offer you an additional insurance policy for your festival event scheduled for May thirteenth through fifteenth of the current year. This event cancellation insurance protects revenues and expenses against the risks of cancellation, postponement, or reduction in attendance of the event for reasons beyond the control of the event organizer. The policy is an 'all-cause' coverage and can protect against severe weather conditions, venue unavailability (due to fires, floods, and power outages), threats or acts of terrorism, earthquakes, wildfires, labor strikes, non-appearance of a key person and more.

"I wonder if murder is covered?"

April shrugged. "Maybe it is considered an act of terrorism?"

"Or would be under the non-appearance of a key person," I mused. "I mean, she appeared before, but now…not so much." I read the policy information again.

"This includes reduced attendance," I noticed. "Meaning if there is a significant reduction in attendance due to the above-listed circumstances, the insured will be protected."

"How much is the policy for?" April asked.

I scrolled down. "Looks like one million dollars."

"Made out to him personally?"

"I don't think any insurance company would do that. The town is listed on the policy, so they'd receive the money."

"That would be a lot of money for a small town." April returned to the folder on the table and sifted through the documents. "Especially since it would go solely to Redding Beach. The contracts with the vendors offer no such cancellation policy. It indemnifies the town from any fault if the event is cancelled or reduced. The town would totally win if any of the days got cancelled. Probably more than if the event went off without any problems."

"Sounds like a motive for murder to me," I said. "And if he offed Erica as well, he'd personally gain two million."

April shook her head. "I *still* say it would not be worth it for the negative publicity from Heather's death, or in the worst-case scenario, from the death of Heather, Erica, and you."

I shuddered at the thought. "Maybe he didn't care about the long-term effect since the short-term would be profitable. Anyway, we shouldn't stay too long. Let me look at the rest of the emails."

In the quiet of the office, I could hear the spinning and clicking of the mouse as I scrolled through. "No. I can see where he hired additional security after Heather's death, and he plays up how concerned he is for his judges, chefs, and attendees."

"Has to be shown doing his due diligence," April guessed.

"And lots of email exchanges with vendors, chefs, and concerned citizens, stating what steps he is taking to ensure the safety and success of this event." More clicking and scrolling as I checked further. "I could do this for hours, but I don't see anything too suspicious. Let me check the drive."

April returned the festival folder to the file cabinet, then searched the other drawers. She called out a few minutes later. "Employee files. Interesting. Erica is an employee of the town. He has her listed as a consultant for the crab festival. Not a bad hourly rate either."

"So the Wheeler family will benefit personally from this festival, regardless of the outcome." I kept looking through the computer but didn't find anything particularly damning. I jumped when my cell phone dinged.

"Really?" April glared. "You did not silence your phone?"

"It's not like we're at the library," I protested as I read the text. "And it's Daniel. He's been released but told not to leave town. He's not sure if they're going to press charges against him."

I texted him that we'd meet him at the hotel. "Let's clean up." I pulled up my photos and made certain nothing looked disturbed. April moved the keyboard two centimeters to the right, and we were good.

When we entered the foyer, I re-alarmed the building. I put in the code, then hesitated when I had to choose between Stay and Away. "Stay is so the motion detectors don't work when you remain in the house," I said to April, recalling it from my own alarm system. I pushed the Away button. "I hope that's the one they usually choose."

I was glad for the tinted windows as we peeked out to see if anyone was on the road. Not seeing anyone, we slipped out the door and back to the hotel.

When Jessica opened the door to Daniel's hotel room, I was immediately concerned. Daniel sat at his desk, his hands pressed against his temples as he stared morosely at the laptop screen.

She stepped into the hallway with us and closed the door.

"What's going on?" I whispered to Jessica. "Is it worse than he let on?"

She shook her head and sighed quietly. "It's not the murder. The police accused him of faking the contract as a cover for researching cyanide. It turns out the publishing company that offered him a contract is a scam company."

"Oh, how sad," April said.

Jessica nodded. "I'm not certain if he's upset that the company is a scam, which means his book won't be published, or if he's upset that he almost fell for a scam."

"Probably both," I said. "He's always on me about avoiding scams and security risks and everything. And he was so happy his book was going to be published."

"It didn't help that he emailed Detective Preston the manuscript in order to prove that he did, in fact, write an entire book. When it was suggested that he might have written the book as a cover, I pointed out that deleting the search history off your computer would have been much easier, especially for a man of Daniel's background, than writing an entire novel. After a short break, the detective returned and told Daniel he must be telling the truth about the book since no one would deliberately write a book that bad. Daniel was angry and about to react, which was the detective's intent, but I called for a moment to consult with my client."

I felt horrible for my brother.

"That was an unkind thing for Detective Preston to say," April said, frowning. "Did you defend him?"

"Aunt April," Jessica said quietly. "I'm more concerned with defending him against a murder charge. Again, they have no real evidence, but it's a lot. Daniel admitted he had threatened Simon with murder if he cheated but said he hadn't been serious. Then there's all the research about cyanide and the fact that he did disappear during the tasting."

"He was taking a phone call," I protested. "Wouldn't phone records show the incoming call?"

"Phone records take forever to subpoena, and since the publishing company is a scam anyway, their calling doesn't prove anything. Detective Preston also kept saying that a savvy young computer expert wouldn't have fallen for a scam. I don't know. They might charge him."

"It's all circumstantial," I said, calling on all my legal knowledge, mostly based on television shows and movies.

"It is. That doesn't prevent the police from pressing charges." Jessica opened the door again.

Daniel was still in the same position.

I crouched next to him, thankful for my stretchy leggings. "I'm sorry, Daniel, about the book."

He turned to me and sighed. "Me too. I was so excited that it blinded me to reality. I *know* better. If something seems too easy, there's a reason behind it. I feel so stupid. Especially since I know this isn't what I should be worried about. I should be worried about being arrested for murder."

"We might be able to help with that." I stood and turned to Jessica. "Can we provide an anonymous tip to the police that they should check the mayor's insurance policies? He just took out a two-million-dollar one on his wife and a million-dollar policy for the festival."

"How do you know that?" Jessica asked in stereo with Daniel.

Then Daniel threw his hands up. "Tell me you didn't break into the mayor's office."

Jessica held out a hand. "Wait. Really don't tell me. Not yet. Jackie, I'm still your lawyer too, so that's okay." She turned to April. "But not yours…yet. Since you're with her and dressed like that when there's no funeral in sight, I'm going to guess I'm your lawyer also."

After April nodded, Jessica took a deep breath. "Okay, tell me."

We told them of our break-in and the investigative discoveries.

"Talking about circumstantial, that's all you have too," Jessica said when we were finished. "Also, don't go breaking into government buildings! They probably have you on camera."

I shook my head. "No, I didn't see cameras yesterday. It's an old building, and I wouldn't be surprised if the town can't afford them. I checked again today before our foray into breaking and entering."

Jessica pinched her eyes closed. "Did you forward yourself any of this information? Take pictures of the insurance documents?"

April and I looked at each other. I cleared my throat. "That...that would probably have been smart. But then there'd be a record of it in his email."

"You'd delete the forward, Jackie," Daniel said. He copied Jessica's eye-closing expression. "And there'd be no record if you had taken photos."

"This was my first break-in, okay?" I said, putting my hands on my hips. "They didn't teach us this in culinary school. Besides, the cops should be able to find proof of the insurance policies, at least."

Jessica tilted her head in acknowledgment. "They could subpoena the insurance company's records. Still—and I'm not saying there should be a next time—but get proof next time."

"You're still encouraging her, Jessica," Daniel said. "I appreciate you taking the risk for my sake, but don't do it again."

"Oh!" April exclaimed, her gaze fixed on the alarm clock perched on the nightstand. "It is almost four o'clock! Just an hour left until the tasting. I must get ready." Without another word, she dashed out the door.

"Prepare for what?" Jessica asked. "Is she up to something else?"

"Don't look at me," I said when she and Daniel did so. "Maybe she has to pick the perfect 'watching a food contest' outfit."

chapter nineteen
. . .

"AND IT'S FINALLY HERE!" Mayor Tom yelled into the microphone quite unnecessarily. "Time for freestyle crab. Who's ready to get crabby?"

I raised an eyebrow at Erica. "I think after this weekend, we're all crabby."

She quietly laughed.

The crowd had grown today. Some of them might even have been there to enjoy the festival, to spend money in town, and not just drawn here for the possibility of witnessing murder.

I sighed. Or perhaps I was a bit cynical. There were people I knew who didn't want another death and were here to support the chefs. My brother was here to support me, which was so amazing considering his own worries. Jessica was here as well. I hoped this time didn't count toward her fee. Although, honestly, it was worth it if it made Daniel feel better to have her there.

In the next row up, I was glad to see Skylar. Evidently, her parents hadn't insisted she leave and were letting her attend the tasting. I could see an older woman I presumed was her tutor sitting next to her, glancing around the audience like she suspected we were out to kill her student.

I couldn't quite blame her. I had to admit I was treating everyone like a suspect too.

I still thought it was the mayor. The two insurance policies, both newly purchased, would mean that if Erica had died, the mayor would have made two million, and the town would have made a million, making the mayor look…good? I mean, it would make him look prepared and responsible, but cancelling the festival he had been promoting so heavily seemed counterproductive. And although he might profit this year, he'd have trouble next year with his "annual" festival. Vendors and chefs would probably not want to participate in a cursed event.

So maybe it wasn't him. Then who?

I couldn't see Skylar as the killer either. She seemed so forthright and honest in all of our conversations. If she had killed someone, I think she would have come right out and admitted to it.

Benjy couldn't be the murderer. Like April had said about how she couldn't see the mayor poisoning his own well, I definitely couldn't see Benjy poisoning his own soup. That would have and did have negative repercussions to his life, to his business. Which reminded me that I needed to ask him if reservations had rebounded or if more people had cancelled.

I did spot someone I wouldn't mind being the killer and ending up in prison. For some reason, Simon was in attendance. He was pointedly not looking at me. Fine with me.

I moved on to the other chefs. After her casual discussion about the Pastry Incident and lack of anger, I was fairly confident Veronica wasn't the killer. At least, I couldn't think of a motive she would have to kill any of us.

Seeing Greg with his camera, I wondered about his motives. He had worked with Heather, who, from all the rumors I had heard, was horrible to work with. I could easily see her berating someone she would just think of as crew, as a lowly employee.

When the first contestant walked up, I stopped my potential killer analysis to focus on food. Especially since this was yesterday's winner, Sofia Delgado. Her avocado crab cake had been delicious, so I looked forward to today's entry.

She approached the table, placed three bowls in front of us, and smiled sweetly. At least, she looked sweet, but could she have been the killer? Heather had been horrid to her. "Today I have for you Jaiba Ceviche. Jaiba"—she pronounced it hy-ba—"is the Spanish word for blue crab, specifically. I have provided freshly made tortilla chips for dipping."

The dish was bright and beautiful. I could see green flecks of jalapeño, gorgeous red tomatoes, bright-orange mango, white lumps of crab, chunks of onion—why were red onions called that when they are clearly purple?

Once again, it was time for the judges' game of chicken. I was feeling brave, so I picked up a chip. Erica did the same, but Mayor Tom was staring at the dish like it was a loaded bomb. Erica nudged him.

"What?" he asked. "Oh, I'm not worried about poison. It's just...isn't ceviche raw? Like eating sushi?" The way he said eating sushi would be like me saying eating mud.

"Oh, do not worry," Sofia said. "Although often ceviche does use raw fish, the use of the lime juice denatures the fish."

He looked at her blankly.

"The acid basically cooks it, dear," Erica explained, her voice full of long-suffering patience.

"Yes," Sofia agreed. "But in this case, with crab, you don't need to worry about it. I started out with already cooked lump crab meat."

Seemingly satisfied, the mayor shoved a chip into the bowl, breaking the chip in two. He grabbed another one and successfully loaded up a chip. Then he paused and waited, probably for one of us to try first.

I scooped a generous portion onto a chip, making sure to grab some of each component. The flavor exploded in my mouth. Very citrusy, which paired so well with the sweetness of the crab. And the tortilla was perfectly executed and a great vessel for the ceviche.

"Very bright," I said after quickly swallowing. That was always the hardest part of judging, the need to offer your opinion quickly without speaking with your mouth full. "Such a nice complement to the crab. The sweetness of the crab is punched up from the acid from the mango, lime, and...lemon," I hazarded a guess. She nodded.

"And it's beautiful," Erica said. "They always say that you eat with your eyes first."

"Might be a bad idea with something this acidic," I joked. "Would sting."

A flicker of annoyance passed over Erica's face and was gone. "But Jackie is right. The acid does add so much to the sweet." She turned to Tom. "What do you think?"

I braced myself for another "Yummy."

"I also liked the combination of all the ingredients. Quite flavorful," he said.

I raised an eyebrow at Erica. She leaned in and whispered, "We worked on this last night."

Sofia stepped away happily.

Next up was Veronica. She placed black oval plates in front of us. The ebony-colored ceramic set off the food, a cream-based sauce over pasta, just brimming with lump crab.

"I have prepared for you Crab Alfredo, a favorite at Pasta n' Boots. In honor of the crab, in addition to the velvety cream sauce, we also added Chesapeake seasoning for a little heat." Veronica bobbed her head and stepped back. "Buon Appetito," she added, combining an Italian accent with a Texas drawl.

Mayor Tom picked up his fork quickly this time, probably happy to try something more familiar to him. He did lose any points he'd gained from the prior professional-sounding food critique by asking Veronica for a spoon. At least he didn't ask her for a knife to cut the pasta.

The fettuccine was textbook perfect, and she had accurately described the sauce. It was velvety and smooth. "I'll give you credit for risking a cream-based sauce on a hot Texas day," I said, gesturing with a fork.

She laughed. "I was terrified it would break, honestly."

A broken sauce was one of a chef's fears. A beautifully emulsified sauce separating into liquids and oils was something we'd all had happen, often at the worst times.

"Nicely done," Erica agreed. "I also liked the addition of Old B— sorry, Chesapeake seasoning. It added a little kick to the pasta."

Mayor Tom shook his head. "This is Texas. When you say heat, I expect *heat*. I could barely taste any spice."

Erica placed a hand on his arm. "You wouldn't want too much spice with such a delicate sauce. It would overpower it."

He frowned. "I'll take your word for it since you're the expert. But I still think a little Tabasco sauce would…brighten it up."

When Veronica returned to her previous spot, the mayor ran up to the podium.

"Thanks to some…unexpected withdrawals from the contest, we had some openings and a last-minute contestant stepped up," Mayor Tom said with obvious pride and excitement in his voice. I had to smile when I saw the surprise contestant. The woman was amazing. I don't know how she had managed to both prepare food for today's contest *and* help me snoop in Town Hall.

Mayor Tom beamed. "April Yao came all the way from San Francisco, California, to compete in Redding Beach. Obviously, word has gotten around."

I didn't disagree, but I suspected those words involved "potential murder" or "stay the hell away."

"Thank you, Mayor Thomas," April said with her usual precise diction as she placed three plates down gracefully. I admired her gorgeous chef's coat, a sharp red with a black embroidered dragon. "I have prepared for you Crab and Scallion Pancakes."

"Pancakes," Mayor Tom asked. "With crab? And where's the syrup?"

Erica nudged him. "It's a savory dish, Tom. Please finish, Chef April."

"Thank you. This is blue crab meat seasoned with Texas chili spices and chopped scallions, folded into savory Taiwanese-style pancakes combining the tastes of Taiwan, China, and Texas." She bowed and backed away from the table.

"It had better be spicy," the mayor said.

When I tasted her dish, I smiled. "That's not going to be a problem, Mayor Tom. There's definitely heat. And it's amazing. The pancakes are golden and crispy on the outside, yet tender inside with the freshness of the scallions, and the crab meat is so succulent."

Erica hummed quietly in pleasure before swallowing. "I agree. It's like a harmonious blend of indulgence and satisfaction."

The mayor picked up his water glass and took a deep gulp. "And it does have some spice, little lady. Thank you."

Last up was Benjy. This put him at a disadvantage due to following April's delicious but very spicy offering.

Benjy placed the three plates on the table, and I saw I had guessed correctly about his entry. There was a stack of four perfectly round and perfectly browned croquettes. The shape was closer to a pyramid than a tower since he had three orbs on the bottom and one on top. I could see a dark caramel had been used to adhere the croquettes and also drizzled artfully on the food.

"I present a crab croquembouche." At Erica's shocked expression, he hurried to explain. "It's a savory version, featuring crab and corn croquettes and a fish sauce caramel with black and red pepper to offset the sweetness."

That seemed to soothe Erica's concerns, but Mayor Tom still looked worried. I wasn't certain if that was due to the unusual food or if he was still suspicious of Benjy.

Not wanting to look timid about eating Benjy's food, I rushed to take a bite and regretted it immediately. Even though Benjy was the last contestant, potatoes were incredible at keeping their temperature. I ended up burning the top of my mouth.

It was worth the pain. The croquette was even better than the one I'd had this morning. The fish sauce caramel surprisingly matched it.

"This is amazing," I said. "I had wondered if the fish sauce caramel would be too sweet, but salt and spice were the more forward tastes."

"I agree the caramel sauce works," Erica said. "But I would think if you're going to describe this as a croquembouche, it should be made of profiteroles, not croquettes."

Here I ended up disagreeing with her. "Croquembouche and croquette both come from the French word for crunchy." I took a bite for emphasis, heard the crackle. "This qualifies. I'd say as long as it's a round thing you can stack in a tower and it's crunchy, it works."

"This is a tower?" Erica asked, indicating her plate.

"I didn't want to overwhelm you with too many croquettes," Benjy said calmly, his voice free of defensiveness.

Erica looked like she was going to protest again, but Mayor Tom jumped in. "It's definitely unique. I thought I'd hate it, but actually…" He took another croquette and shoved it in his mouth before standing and heading to the podium.

"Fank you—" He stopped, swallowed. "Thank you, chefs, for your amazing creations. Please give me and my lovely co-judges some time to debate. Y'all have definitely made this decision difficult."

Erica and I stood and met Tom outside the tent. We huddled together.

"I hate to say it," Tom said, "but I liked Benjy's the most."

"Absolutely not," Erica protested. "It wasn't a croquembouche. That is supposed to be a pastry dish, and that wasn't pastry."

"I think it was very creative," I said.

"Creativity on its own doesn't have much merit when the dish is just too odd," Erica said firmly. "Not croquembouche."

"And we probably don't want to award the best prize to Benjy until they find out who killed Heather," Tom said.

I was outnumbered. "Fine, but Benjy deserves second." I glared at Tom. "And really give him second this time."

"Of course. Of course. Who should take first then? I liked Sofia's," Tom said.

"The flavors were delicious," I agreed. "But she didn't actually cook anything. Even the crab meat was already cooked when she started with it."

Erica nodded. "Although she did make incredible tortilla chips."

"I think her family would disown her if she didn't," I said. "But this is a crab festival, not a tortilla chip festival."

"I was certain I'd love the fettuccine alfredo," Mayor Tom said. "But I think she needed to cook the pasta more. It was too chewy."

"What?" I protested. "It was perfectly al dente. That means 'to the tooth' for a reason. I thought it was the correct texture."

"As did I," Erica said. "I had to learn to overcook pasta for Tom, or he would always complain. I die a little each time I do that to good pasta."

"I also wish it had been spicier since she promised spicy."

"No," I said to Tom. "She said a little heat."

"It was very little."

Erica shook her head. "Ignoring that, I think Veronica's dish was a strong contender. The sauce was perfect, which is hard to do in an outdoor kitchen."

"Yes, but there's nothing creative about a seafood alfredo," I protested.

Erica inclined her head in agreement. "Good point."

"If you want a creative dish," I began. "You can't get more creative than Benjy's."

My other two judges shook their heads in disagreement.

"I have to say April's crab pancake things were both creative and delicious," Mayor Tom said. "And while I'd prefer to award a Texan chef, it is rather prestigious to have a chef of her caliber and fame win our little contest."

"So…do we think it's April, then Benjy, then Sofia?" I asked.

Erica looked between me and her husband, then nodded. "I'm still annoyed at him calling it a croquembouche, but it *was* unique and delicious. It's April, then Benjy, then Sofia. No changes this time, Tom."

"No changes," he promised.

The crowd quieted as he stepped on stage.

"There was certainly stiff competition today for freestyle crab," the mayor began. "We've been arguing over who was the best, and it was a hard fight, but me and the girls finally figured it out."

Erica and I both winced at the word "girls."

"In third place, teaching me that ceviche is better than sushi, we have Sofia Delgado."

Sofia started crying as she walked up to take her prize. I hoped they were tears of joy, but after Benjy's talk about her losing her restaurant, they might be tears of sorrow.

"In second place, with a savory interpretation of…" He looked at Erica. "How do you say it, honey?"

"Croquembouche," Erica said through gritted teeth.

"Right, croquembouche, we have Benjy Hayes."

Benjy was satisfied as he took his prize. Since I watched him when he walked back, I saw him slip it over to Sofia. She shook her head at him, bowed her head low, then took the envelope.

"And in first place, our surprise entry, April Yao from Little Dragon in San Francisco. Thank you, April."

A surge of pride and gratitude filled me as I witnessed April claim her prize, only to also pass it along to Sofia.

chapter twenty

. . .

"I DON'T THINK I'm going to want crab for years," I said.

Erica patted her stomach. "That makes two of us. Every bite was delicious, but there's such a thing as too much of a good thing."

I paused. "It feels wrong to say this, but it's been a pleasure to judge this with you. I mean, other than what happened Friday night. But you have very good taste."

Erica glanced over at her husband and grimaced. "In most things, that is."

I grinned. "Okay, let's say you have good tasting ability. You could taste the nuances, knew what made good food. Not bad for an amateur." I stood and walked to where my friends were gathered. Benjy, Skylar, and Daniel were congratulating April on her win.

"What did you just say to Erica?" Skylar asked immediately.

"I told her I was impressed at her tasting ability. Why?"

"After you turned around, she looked very upset." Skylar stared at Erica. "Her nostrils flared, she tilted her chin up, and dug her nails into her palms."

"I definitely didn't mean to upset her," I said, turning back to the judging table where the mayor had joined his wife.

"Oh, Jackie," Tom said. "I can't thank you enough for not only bringing some celebrity status to our judging but also for sticking with us, despite the…difficulties."

He did have a way with understatement. "I'm working on keeping my promises. And not offending people. Erica, did I say something wrong before? Skylar thought you looked upset."

Erica blinked a few times. "No. I was fine. I looked upset? My stomach might be, from all this food. Maybe that's what Skylar saw."

"Oh, I'm glad. Well, please keep me in mind for next year's crab festival."

"Yes, the second Annual Redding Beach Crab Festival." The mayor glanced around. "Hopefully, there will be more contestants."

"And fewer…difficulties," I said.

Tom held out a hand to help Erica stand. "And thank you, dear, for all your help." He smiled at me while holding his wife's hand. "My wife really did all the hard work. She handled the PR and took care of all the contracts. She even managed all of my emails. I'm hopeless with technology."

Erica smiled, shaking her head. Her blouse shifted, revealing a delicate gold necklace.

"That's a gorgeous necklace. Where did you get it?"

Erica beamed. "Actually, I made it. I design and create jewelry and also do some restoration work."

"Yes, it's her little hobby," Tom said, pulling her with him toward the exit.

This time I noticed Erica's nostrils flare. I walked back to my friends, feeling bad that Erica's husband was so dismissive of her crafting work. *Little hobby*. Working with jewelry couldn't be easy.

I stopped dead in my tracks.

Erica worked with jewelry.

I rushed back to the group, ran up to Daniel. "Didn't you say potassium cyanide is often used by jewelers?"

Daniel nodded. "Yeah, it's used for cleaning. Why?"

"Erica works with jewelry." I turned around, spotting Erica and Mayor Tom talking to one of the sponsors.

"That doesn't necessarily mean she'd have potassium cyanide, but—"

I rushed on. "You notice she also didn't taste the soup immediately, waiting while Heather tried it."

"Neither did you," Benjy said, but his eyes gleamed. "What motive would she have?"

"I don't know." My excitement deflated slightly. "I don't even know her maiden name." I whipped out my phone and checked Facebook to see if she had accepted my friend request. She still hadn't.

"Knopfler," Daniel said, glancing up from his own phone. "I found their wedding announcement."

"Erica Knopfler," I said. "Why does that sound familiar?"

"I agree," Benjy said.

Veronica, who'd been at the next table, popped over. "Oh, you remembered her name!"

I turned around slowly and stared at Veronica. "What do you mean?" I asked.

"The Pastry Incident. It was Erica Knopfler whose croquembouche you destroyed."

"Uh-oh," Skylar said. "She heard that."

I spun around. Erica was staring at our group. She pivoted and sprinted out of the tent.

It took a second for all of us to realize what had happened.

"I'll go tell the police," Skylar and April said at the same time.

Benjy, Daniel, and I raced out of the tent, leaving Veronica in the dust. Poor thing probably had no idea why we'd all reacted like that.

I saw Erica sprinting down the boardwalk. Remembering how fast she was, I wondered if any of us would be able to catch her. Benjy was injured from the dog chase, and I'd always been a faster runner than my brother. It was on me.

Erica craned her neck back and noticed we were following her. As she ran over a bridge that spanned an inlet, she shoved a teenage girl into the water. I almost stopped, but knowing the others behind me could help, I figured my goal was to catch Erica.

We kept running straight past the long parking lot. She rammed into another person, knocking their bags of popcorn, candy, and souvenirs onto the ground. I leaped over it all and tried to gain any ground on her. This felt as helpless as chasing the corgi. That reminded me!

I could see the right turn up ahead. Searching for the broken fencing, I saw it at the last minute and jumped. Certain I had just made a stupid decision, I was totally surprised when I cleared the broken section, saying a quick thanks to Benjy's error. I raced across the parking lot and ducked between two buildings.

I stepped out in front of her, right in the same place we had caught the dog. She was going too fast to stop, so she crashed into me, taking both of us painfully to the ground.

I scrambled to my knees, worried she'd escape, but thankfully, Daniel had her back on her feet and had trapped her arms behind her. Benjy reached out a hand. I took it gratefully, and he raised me up. All sorts of bruises made themselves known to me as I stood.

"You okay?" Benjy asked, concern on his face.

"Will be. But for right now, let me just say ow."

chapter twenty-one

. . .

AS WE STOOD THERE, Erica struggling, a mob of people arrived on the scene.

When Skylar and April arrived, with Greg right behind them, I limped over to my friends. "Are the police on the way? Did you tell them?"

April nodded her head. "Yes. They have just stopped to help that poor girl who fell in the water."

I glanced over at Greg, who had his camera up and presumably filming. I wondered how much of the chase he'd managed to capture.

"What's going on?" Mayor Tom asked, running up, out of breath.

I pointed at his wife. "Erica added the poison."

He snorted. "No way. Why would she ruin my festival?"

"I don't know that answer," I said. "But I know why she went after me and Heather. The Pastry Incident."

Erica firmed her lips, not responding.

Mayor Tom looked more confused than ever. "What is the Pastry Incident? A new restaurant or something?"

"Your wife was in culinary school with us. But she was Erica Knopfler then. Heather was mad at me and pushed me into Erica's croquembouche tower, ruining it."

Mayor Tom's look of confusion turned to recognition. "I've heard that story. She dropped out of culinary school because of that."

"No," Erica said, evidently unable to stay silent. "It wasn't just the croquembouche. Heather and Jackie were my reason for dropping out. They were perfect. Not because they were great chefs but because they were gorgeous. No one else received any attention from the faculty, other than Benjy, who had all the female instructors favoring him.

"I hated both of you, and neither of you even noticed me. That tower was the last straw," Erica took a quick breath. "Pastry was the one subject where I was better than any of you. My croquembouche tower was my crowning glory, and I had spent hours on it. Hours!" she spit out, with actual spittle included.

I didn't need Skylar's help to read the body language. Her red face, bulging eyes, and harsh words were pretty big clues that she was beyond angry. I'd seen my fair share of people passionate about food, but this seemed deranged.

"So you arranged all of this?" I asked.

Deranged, maybe, but apparently not stupid enough to confess. She pressed her lips tightly again.

I shifted my attention to the mayor. "Why did you invite me to judge this festival?"

He glanced at his wife and cleared his throat. "Erica suggested it. Mentioned you were down on your luck but still famous enough to be a draw. She said I could get you for cheap."

"She knew how to work you, didn't she?" I asked. "And then I bet she let Heather know I was going to be a judge."

Mayor Tom swallowed. "She sent out press releases to a number of chefs. She said it was a way to entice them to compete."

"It worked," Benjy said. "I admit I decided to compete, in part, to see you."

I stared into his intense blue eyes, then shook my head. This was not a time to get into that. "And it obviously worked on Heather as well since she couldn't resist offering her services as a stab at me."

"I was just doing my job," Erica said, defending herself.

"Right, your job." I turned back to the mayor. "Talking about that, the jewelry she makes. Her 'little hobby.' She said she restores jewelry as well?"

He nodded, looking like a deer caught in the headlights. "She does. She creates custom jewelry but also cleans people's antique items. Why is that important?"

"I know. I know!" Skylar said. "That's one use for potassium cyanide."

Daniel nodded. "She had the means, she had the motive, and she had the opportunity."

Erica scowled but didn't say anything.

"But Erica would never do this to me," Mayor Tom said. "She knows how important this festival is to me, right, dear? Tell them they're wrong."

She pinched her eyes closed. I could see the blood rushing back up her face, but she wasn't budging.

"This festival couldn't have happened if it wasn't for her," he continued. "She was my adviser, my PR, everything. Because she was a cook and understood the ins and outs."

"Chef!" Erica blurted out. "A chef!"

"Right, right." He nodded nervously. "A chef."

"She was?" I asked.

"She was when we met. Was a sow chef or something like that," he said.

"Sous," Erica barked out.

"Sous chef. But she gave that all up when we married, so she could help promote my political career."

"Your precious career!" Erica snapped out. "That's all that matters to you. I quit my own career to support you. And that's after I changed my entire life for you to even notice me, dyed my hair, changed to contacts, and lost weight."

"That's probably better for your health, dear."

"Don't dear me," Erica said, losing it again. "You don't care about my health. You don't care about me. Just your damn career. You even said you only married me to advance your political career. That's when I decided to ruin you by—" She stopped when she noticed the police approaching. "Not that I did. This is all just conjecture. You can't prove anything."

"Maybe not in a court of law. But I bet the court of public opinion will be convinced." I pointed at Greg.

Her mouth dropped. "You're recording?" She must have been so focused on me that she hadn't noticed Greg and his camera.

"Yup," Greg answered. "Never expected to record an action chase scene for the Gourmet Channel."

"What's going on here?" Detective Preston asked as he pushed through the crowd. "Why did one of you shove that girl into the inlet? She's okay, fortunately, but the family is already saying they want to press charges."

"Arrest her," I said, pointing at Erica.

"I've got it on video if you'd like." Greg hefted his camera for emphasis.

"And not just for the shove," I added. "But for Heather's murder." I quickly explained all our evidence against Erica. The detective was dubious at first but seemed convinced by the time I was finished detailing the facts.

"You have the assault on video?" Detective Preston asked Greg.

He nodded. "Yeah, I turned it on and followed when I saw everyone booking from the tent." He fiddled with the camera, then turned it around so that Preston could see the preview window.

Preston watched without comment, then asked if he could take the camera for evidence. "We'll return it once we download the footage, but this also prevents you from releasing this to the media. It's best if we can delay that a while." He then turned to Erica. "Mrs. Wheeler, you are under arrest for the assault on the Hanner family. Additional charges may come after we review the recording and from further testimony with these witnesses." He hesitated, then drew out his handcuffs. He took her by the wrists. "I'd appreciate it if the rest of you could come to the police station to formally provide this information."

"Veronica Rossi should come as well," I said. "She also knew Erica at culinary school."

"That would be good." Preston walked away, Erica by his side.

Officers Short and Tall followed. After a momentary hesitation, the mayor walked behind them as well.

The rest of the group then turned to face me. Daniel was the first to go for a hug. "Detective Jackie, for the win!"

Almost everyone else followed suit with lots of compliments and congratulations.

April held me at arm's length after her hug. "I am so grateful you did not immediately taste the food. If you had, Erica might have been able to kill two birds with one soup."

I laughed but felt a shiver go up my spine at the idea.

Benjy's hug was long. "Thank you for clearing my name. I'm sure once this information gets out—and the police won't be able to keep a lid on it for long—the public will forget all about whose soup it was, and all the attention will be on Erica. I suppose, in some ways, that's what she's always wanted."

Greg held up his phone. "She's already got it. There's no way the police can suppress this. Other people have already uploaded footage of the chase from their phones, and there's lots of conjecture that the mayor's wife must be the killer. Great job figuring that out." It was his turn to give me a hug. That sent a shiver up my spine for a far more pleasant reason.

chapter twenty-two
. . .

AFTER A CRAZY SUNDAY evening and an even crazier Monday, Daniel and I were packed and ready to get away from this crazy town. I had said goodbye and many, many thank-yous to April the day before, who had decided that because all crises were averted, she could return to California.

We were on our way to do the same. As I wheeled my luggage down to the lobby, carrying my laptop bag with my released-from-the-police laptop, I saw Skylar checking out. I raced over. "Thank you so much, Skylar," I said. "You were key in helping me spot Erica as the killer. I couldn't have done it without your ability to decipher body language."

She smiled shyly. "My parents might say that's the first time anyone ever said they were thankful for my neurodivergence."

"Your parents are wrong," I said firmly. "About pursuing a career in the culinary field, too, in my humble opinion. I'm sure you'd be a great chef."

The smile grew wider.

"Are you comfortable with hugging?" I asked. I noticed she hadn't hugged me on Sunday after the crazy chase scene.

"Thank you for asking," she said, shrinking away ever so slightly. "I'd prefer not to, honestly, but if you insist, I will."

I shook my head. "Fist bump?"

"Fist bump is good." We exchanged one. She nodded toward the lobby, where I could see Greg and Benjy sitting near each other. "And talking about body language, they're both exhibiting a number of emotions. Admiration, which is obvious because they keep leaning forward in your direction, watching your moves, and adjusting their shirts. Plus, they're showing signs of jealousy toward each other: crossing their arms in front of their chest, which then requires adjusting their shirts again, tightening their arm and chest muscles. I think they have romantic intentions toward you."

I laughed, gave her another fist bump, and walked over to my admiring, jealous men. They both stood as I approached. I slowed down as I got closer. Whom should I talk to first?

Greg solved my indecision by stepping forward. Benjy frowned at his back.

"Heading out?" he asked.

"We are," I said, noticing Daniel had stepped out of the elevator. Unfortunately, Simon also stepped out. I ignored Simon and turned to Greg. "You?"

"The Thursday flight was cheaper, so Gourmet Channel has me traveling to some restaurants in the area." He sighed. "I'm glad I've got other work with them since I've lost the gig on *The Clean Cook*."

"I hope they find something for you soon. If they ever do revive *Dinner, Drinks, and Decadence*, I'll request you. But I suspect I've got a while to go before the Gourmet Channel trusts me again." I couldn't blame them. I was still struggling to trust myself. "But I do have a couple of festivals coming. A frog legs festival in Louisiana in July and a mushroom festival in Maryland in September."

He grimaced. "I'll pass on the frog legs, but I'll see if I can cover the mushroom festival. The one in Kennett Square?"

I shook my head. "I'm not invited to the big, established festivals. This is a somewhat new one in a small town called Conway."

"See you in Maryland then." Aware that Benjy was waiting and watching, I gave Greg a quick hug and then turned to my ex-boyfriend.

"I know what happened this weekend was due to the misdeeds of the past," I started. "But I'm glad we were able to settle our issues. At least, I hope we did. I'm very sorry I didn't trust you ten years ago."

"And I'm sorry I didn't fight harder for you." He blew out a breath that had a tinge of frustration in it. "But hopefully, we can work past that and learn to be friends again." His warm glance made me wonder if Skylar was right. "Hopefully, you'll have another festival or other gig near Houston. And I might have more time myself."

I gasped. "Your restaurant is still doing horribly?"

"On the contrary, actually. Now that the video came out showing Erica was the guilty party and not me, Kimi's Kitchen is busier than ever." He smiled, then frowned suddenly. "But not so much for Sofia Delgado. Even with the money and attention from this weekend, she'll need to shutter the restaurant. That's a major loss for her, but I think many of us have experienced that."

I laughed. "Many of us have."

"Sorry," he said. "I guess you have experienced that. Hopefully, that will end well for you also. In my case, Sofia's loss is my gain. She's agreed to come back as my sous chef."

"That's great. There's nothing like having a really great second in command. I lost a great sous chef when my restaurant went south. And even more, I feel guilty that my drinking cost him his job."

"Talking about chefs, thank you for introducing me to April Yao." A grin split Benjy's face.

"She is a character," I said, then noticed Daniel pointing toward the clock on the wall. "Anyway, I need to go."

Benjy went for the hug. It felt good. Familiar. I flushed when he added a sweet kiss to my forehead.

"See you around, Benjy," I said, turning around.

I noticed Simon was also waiting for me.

"See you in court," I said, then walked out the front door with Daniel.

"Nice one," my brother said as we exited the hotel.

When we got into the rideshare car, I swiveled into my seat to face him. "So, in all of this craziness, your book got pushed aside. I want to read it. And I'm sorry that the first company didn't work out."

He frowned. "Me too. But I'm glad I found out before I was locked into the contract. And I actually got an email yesterday afternoon from an agent who would like to read through it and offer advice at no charge. I did my research this time, and both the company and the agent, a Mr. Lian Tan, seem quite legit."

April came through again, I realized with a smile. "Well, I'd love to read your novel."

"Talking about love..." Daniel said with a devilish grin. "Who's going to win in this love triangle you've found yourself in? Or is it a love rectangle since you've still got Simon?"

"Simon doesn't count." I rolled my eyes. "And I don't know if anything will happen with Greg or Benjy. Honestly, until my divorce is final and I'm more stable, there's only one man in my life. And that's you."

"That's probably a wise choice. And what about your career? Has the Gourmet Channel reached out to you?"

"Not yet," I said, picking a spot of lint off my pants. "But after this experience, maybe I should pitch a new show to them: *Dinner, Decadence, and Detectives*."

THE END

thank you for reading my book!

. . .

I HOPE you enjoyed your time with Jackie.

Join my mailing list for recipes, foodie news, and updates and as a bonus, receive two more Fatal Food Festival short stories!

www.CathyWileyAuthor.com/subscribe

COMING SOON...

Mushroom Capped - November 29, 2023

Join Jackie Norwood, former celebrity chef and current food festival judge, as she embarks on her latest culinary adventure in *Mushroom Capped,* the tantalizing second installment of the Fatal Food Festival Mystery Series.

Dive into a festival brimming with quirky characters, passionate protestors, and simmering tensions. Conway, once a struggling town, now finds itself at a crossroads: between growth fueled by the mushroom industry and preservation of its small-scale farms and small-town charm. The stakes are high and the locals' convictions run deep and dark… even deadly.

With unexpected twists and turns, *Mushroom Capped* promises a tantalizing mystery that will keep you turning the pages until the very end. Get ready for a savory mix of mystery, community, and mouthwatering cuisine in this delectable cozy mystery.

Grab your apron and magnifying glass; the adventure awaits!

Available November 29, 2023 from major online retailers

recipes

. . .

un-cream of crab soup

1 tablespoon margarine or other butter substitute
2 shallots, minced
2 garlic cloves, minced
1 cup stock (chicken, vegetable, or seafood)
2 cups almond milk
Salt to taste
2 to 3 tablespoons Old Bay or similar seasoning
1 tablespoon tapioca flour (also known as tapioca starch)
2 tablespoons almond butter
1 pound lump crab meat
Additional half pound crab meat (or crab substitute or shrimp)

1. Melt margarine in medium saucepan, add in minced shallots and garlic.
2. Cook until soft, about five minutes.
3. Add in liquids and heat until simmering.

4. Add in Old Bay, salt, and tapioca flour and whisk until lumps are mostly smoothed out.
5. Add in almond butter and the half pound of crab or crab substitute (you will be blending this to make a smooth texture, so not necessary to use lump crab for this), bring to a boil, then reduce to a simmer for five minutes.
6. Use an immersion blender and blend until smooth.
7. Add in lump crab meat and simmer for ten minutes.
8. Serve with additional garnishes like chives or parsley (do not use the additional ingredient used in this book)!

crab croquettes/croquembouche

<u>For Fish Sauce Caramel</u>

1 cup sugar
1 tablespoon fresh lemon juice
¼ cup water
2 tablespoons Asian fish sauce
Black pepper to taste
Red pepper flakes to taste

<u>For Croquettes</u>

1 tablespoon margarine
3 tablespoons shallots, minced
1 cup mashed potatoes (can make fresh, but it should be cold, so leftovers would be perfect)
2 eggs (separated, you will need both whites and yolks)
½ cup corn (cut from fresh corn is best; if frozen, thaw and drain)
½ teaspoon black pepper, or to taste
1 pound of crab meat, hand shredded

1 cup panko breadcrumbs
1 quart canola oil (approximately, as needed for deep frying)

You will need to prepare the caramel sauce first to allow it time to cool and thicken.

1. Combine sugar, lemon juice, and water in a small heavy-bottomed saucepan and bring to a boil. Stir occasionally until it turns a dark amber color and thickens, about 15 minutes. (Be careful of the incredibly hot caramel. Do not touch. Yes, I speak from experience.)
2. Add in fish sauce and whisk. This will loosen the sauce, do not worry. Allow to come to room temperature and it will thicken.

While the caramel is cooling:

1. Melt margarine in medium saucepan, add in minced shallots.
2. Cook until soft, about five minutes. Put into bowl and let come to room temperature.
3. Add in mashed potatoes, egg yolks, corn, black pepper, and crab. Mix, using a spatula or your hands. (They will get messy soon anyway.)
4. Scoop out a golf-ball-sized croquette and roll in your hands into a round ball.
5. Place croquettes on cookie sheet and place in refrigerator to chill for 10 minutes.
6. Preheat the oil in a heavy saucepan. Heat until 350 degrees Fahrenheit.
7. Prep breading station with one bowl with the two egg whites, beaten, and another with the breadcrumbs.
8. Roll the chilled croquettes in the egg whites, then into the breadcrumbs, turning to coat.

9. Return to cookie sheet until all croquettes are done.
10. Using a spider (or tongs, if necessary), gently place the croquettes in the oil in batches of four or five (don't crowd the pan). Fry until golden brown, about two or three minutes. Use the spider to flip them to ensure even browning.
11. Transfer to a plate covered with paper towels.
12. Build "tower" with four croquettes, using a dot of caramel to affix together. Using a spoon, drizzle the caramel over the croquettes and serve immediately.

acknowledgments

It's been over ten years since my last book, and although I've written dozens of short stories in those intervening years, I've forgotten just how much work goes into a full-length novel and just how many people are involved in the process.

I'm deeply thankful to:

- Sharon Cheng, for her unwavering encouragement, exceptional advice, and enduring friendship throughout the years. And to her husband Dean, for his brainstorming and suggestions.
- My husband, Joe, for his love, his endless support, late-night readthroughs, and willingness to assist with everything I needed.
- My brother, David, who was the one who challenged me to finally put the pen to paper (or fingers to the keyboard) and actually write the stories that were in my head.
- To Aubree W., for the tech/TV production advice (any mistakes are mine)
- Ashley H., for her running advice
- My mother, for her encouragement and pride. I wish Dad were here with you to see me reach for my dream.
- Joey and Danelle F., for their late-night taste-testing and creative recipe collaborations.
- Abbie Nicole and Dayna Reidenouer, for their incredible and quick editing skills.

- My critique group members: Becky, Debbi, Lauren, Marcia, Mary Ellen, Rosalie, and Shaun, and my beta reader, Aleta B., for their invaluable insights.
- Lisa Firth of Fully Booked Design in the UK, for the awesome cover.
- The Chessie Chapter Noon Power Writers for their daily encouragement
- Mark Baker, Nikki Bonanni, Dru Ann Love, and Kristopher Zgorski, for their continued support to me and other mystery authors.
- Karen Cantwell, my business partner and friend, whose encouragement and support made this book a reality.
- Tina and Andy P. and all the rest of my friends and family who give me inspiration.

Thank you all from the bottom of my heart for being a part of this journey with me!

about the author

Cathy Wiley is the author of the Fatal Food Festival Mystery Series, featuring a former celebrity chef who's trying to reclaim her career. Three short stories in this series have been published in the Destination Murders anthologies, and the first full-length novel, *Claws of Death*, came out in July. *Mushroom Capped*, the second in the series, comes out in November 2023.

She's also written two other mystery novels set in Baltimore, Maryland, and has had almost a dozen short stories included in anthologies, one of which was a 2015 finalist for a Derringer Award.

She lives outside of Baltimore with one spoiled cat and an equally spoiled husband. For more information, visit www.cathywileyauthor.com.

Join her mailing list and get a free ebook of short stories at www.CathyWileyAuthor.com/subscribe

Printed in Great Britain
by Amazon